HUNTING FOR

DESTINY

A DESTINY TRILOGY
NOVELLA

DERINDA BABCOCK

PUBLISHING THE POSITIVE

ELK LAKE PUBLISHING INC
Plymouth, Massachusetts

Cover and Interior Design: Derinda Babcock

Editor(s): Linda Farmer Harris, Deb Haggerty

PUBLISHED BY: Elk Lake Publishing, Inc., 35 Dogwood Dr., Plymouth, MA 02360, 2018

Library Cataloging Data

Names: Babcock, Derinda (Derinda Babcock)

Hunting For Destiny: A Destiny Trilogy Novella / Derinda Babcock

128 p. 23cm × 15cm (9in × 6 in.)

Identifiers: ISBN-13: 978-1-64949-101-5 (paperback)

| 978-1-64949-102-2 (e-book)

Key Words: Mystery and Sleuthing, Time-travel, Friendship, Pioneer & Oregon Trail, Clean and Wholesome Romance, Family, Relationships

LCCN: 2020949782 Fiction

DEDICATION

To all of you who are hunting for your destiny ...
May you find the joy that passes all understanding.

And the peace of God, which passeth all understanding,

shall keep your hearts and minds through Christ Jesus.

Philippians 4:7 (KJV)

NOTE TO READERS

This story occurs twenty-five years after *In Search of Destiny*, Book Two in the Destiny trilogy. The daughters of Jesse and Mary Johnson, Sean and Annie West, Dwight and Josie Bell, and Jonathan and Olivia Johnson are old enough to realize their folks are hiding information about the mystery woman known as Lexie Logan.

To find out how they met Lexie in Kansas territory, please read the first book in the series, *Dodging Destiny*.

In Search of Destiny, Book Two, follows our characters as they make irrevocable decisions based on what they learned of the future from Lexie.

Book Three, *Following Destiny*, takes us back to the twenty-first century with Lexie to see if, when given another chance, she will run again or face her fears. Lexie learns just how important the people she left in the past were to her existence and her future.

CONTENTS

THE LEGACY CONTINUES ...

Fergus Bell (deceased)
    Jim Bell - Edna
        Mary - Jesse Johnson
            Will, Zach, **LEAH**, Deborah
        Matthew "Mattie"
    Dwight Bell - Josephine "Josie" Aubry (daughter of Alexander)
        Susana
        Polly
        James Fergus Bell
        Grayson Bell

Nathan "Nate" Johnson
    Jonathan - Olivia Aubry (daughter of Phineus)
        Rachel & Sarah (twins)
        Nathaniel Johnson
    Jesse - Mary Bell (see Bell family)

William West
    Benjamin - Laura Shoemaker
        Charles
    Sean - Anne Aubry Taylor (widow—daughter of Alexander)
        BETSY
        Corbin
        David

"When someone you love becomes a memory,
that memory becomes a treasure."
Phil 1:3, Prov. 10:7; Don Jonas 2000.

CHAPTER ONE:

ON THE TRAIL OF A MYSTERY

Oregon, December 1882

Betsy Taylor West
PARENTS: Sean West and Anne Taylor West
SIBLINGS: Corbin and David
UNCLE, AUNT, GRANDFATHER, COUSIN: Benjamin, Laura, William,
Charles

"Shh. Hurry." Betsy West signaled her five friends into her bedroom before glancing down the hall both ways and closing the door.

"Where's Leah?" Sarah Johnson looked at her twin, Rachel, and then toward the door. "We can't start without her."

Betsy grinned. "She's washing up and changing her clothes. Mary told her she smelled like horse and gave her *the look.*"

Rachel giggled. "What did Leah do?"

"She smiled and said, 'Don't worry, Ma, I'll be ready for the Christmas party,' then tromped up the stairs in her boots and spurs."

Susana Bell stared at her reflection in the long mirror and straightened the lace at her throat and wrists. "Aunt Mary always gives Leah that look. Usually, the look is accompanied by a heavy sigh. After more than seventeen years, you'd think my dear aunt would resign herself to the idea Leah loves horses and riding more than people and parties."

Polly Bell stepped up to the mirror and stood beside her sister. "I think the males in our families encourage her. In my opinion, they always have."

Rachel sat up. "Which males, Polly? Surely you don't think Sean encourages her, do you?"

Betsy rolled her eyes. "Daddy Sean wishes she'd gain a little more polish and start looking for a husband. So does Mother. She's been talking about setting Leah up with my cousin, Charles."

Polly chuckled. "Charles seems like a gentleman. He looks a lot like his father—your uncle, Benjamin. Dr. Benjamin West. Impressive. He's so sophisticated. So is your Aunt Laura. I'm glad your relatives decided to travel all the way from Boston to enjoy Christmas with us."

Betsy grimaced. "I hope Grandpa behaves himself."

Polly looked toward Deborah Johnson, who sat in a comfortable chair.

"What do you think, Deb? Do the men of our families encourage your sister to be horse-mad and focused on things other than matrimony?"

Deborah shrugged and brushed a strand of dark brown hair away from her face. "Leah is Leah. She's had a mind of her own ever since I can remember. Even Will and Zac , though older, look up to her. I think she may influence the men more than they influence her."

"I like your brothers, Deb, especially Will. He reminds me of your pa—full of fun and life." Sarah lowered her eyes. "I'm glad our fathers didn't kill each other during the war."

Deborah nodded. "Me too."

Someone knocked.

"The signal. Leah's here." Betsy opened the door. "Come in."

Leah glanced around, and a slow smile curled the corners of her mouth. "What a pretty picture. You all look festive in your Christmas finery." She tilted her dark head. "Everyone knows Sarah and Rachel are identical twins, but if I didn't know better, I'd say Susana and Polly could pass as twins too. Many might think you were quadruplets."

Betsy laughed. "I agree, but shouldn't you expect something like this when Mother and Aunt Josie are identical twins whose fathers were identical twins? When they're together with Olivia, they could be triplets."

"I suppose." Leah sat on Betsy's hope chest and looked at each person. "What is the latest? Did you discover anything?"

"Not really." Susana frowned. "Polly and I overheard Pa and Sean talking about our mystery woman when they walked to the barn yesterday. We weren't close enough to hear much, but when they saw us, they changed the subject."

"Hmm." Betsy pursed her lips. "Matthew, Edna, and Jim also know something about her. When I entered the kitchen to offer my help, Edna was speaking. She said, 'I wonder what she be a-doin' now? Been twenty-five years, but I sure do miss her.' They saw me, and Edna changed the subject.

"When I waylaid Matthew a couple hours later and asked him about the woman, he winked at me and said his lips were sealed."

Polly flicked an invisible piece of lint. "Seems to me, you're waylaying Uncle Mattie a lot these days."

Heat climbed into Betsy cheeks. "Well, why not? He's a kind, handsome, soft-spoken, black-haired giant who knows how to work. He's honest, and people like him. *I* like him—a lot." She wiggled her eyebrows. "Besides, we have much in common. We traveled the Oregon Trail together, you know."

Deborah laughed. "Yes, Uncle Mattie said when you were born, your hair was so light he thought you were bald."

"Never mind about Uncle Matt." Leah turned to the twins, her brown-eyed gaze intent. "Have you heard anything?"

Rachel tapped her bottom lip and frowned. "A few days ago, Mother didn't know Sarah and I sat in the next room reading. When Josie and Annie stopped by to visit, they chatted about how glad they were transportation had improved so much since their days on the Trail."

Sarah nodded. "We didn't pay much attention until they lowered their voices and laughed about how Mother worried about what Pa's reaction to his first sight of her would be. Rachel and I eased toward the door so we could hear more."

Betsy stared. "Why would Olivia fear Jonathan's reaction?"

Sarah frowned. "I'm not sure, but Aunt Josie said she and your mom wondered the same thing. Aunt Josie thought Pa might pass out when he saw them all together. They laughed even harder at Grandpa Nate's words the first time he laid eyes on them. He made some comment about the mystery woman. Then Mother saw us hovering in the doorway and told us to help set the table."

Betsy glanced from Sarah to Rachel and then to Leah. "Do you think they expected Jonathan to be surprised because they are twins? Were twins so uncommon back then?"

Leah shook her head. "I know Uncle Jonathan too well to believe he would be shocked enough by their identical looks to faint unless something else ..."

She pointed to Rachel, Sarah, Susana, and Polly. "All four of you, go and stand by the window and look at me."

Betsy marveled at how quickly the girls obeyed their eldest cousin.

Deborah left the chair and stood next to Leah as they observed their cousins. "Quite impressive, but shocking? Shocking enough to upset our strong-as-a-bull, battle-hardened uncle?"

Betsy waited for Leah to speak. Her friend continued to stare as if she were gazing into the past. "Leah?"

Leah stood and looked from her to her cousins. "We need a plan. We'll never unlock the secrets to this mystery until we stop depending on random encounters with those who knew this mystery woman."

Betsy raised her hand. "I'm in. Where do we start?"

"I think the first thing we need to find out is the woman's name. Once we have this, we can slip her name into our conversations as if we are in the know. We'll see what happens. Unless we tell them otherwise, they'll assume one of the others gave us the information. Be subtle. Don't act curious. Maybe they'll be more willing to tell us more if we don't ask direct questions." Leah looked at each girl. "We need to divide and conquer."

Deborah's smile lit her eyes. "Divide and conquer who or what, Leah?"

"People and information. We need to get our people to talk about their days homesteading and their time on the

Oregon Trail. Something interesting might also come out of the conversation if we can get Pa and Uncle Jon to share their war stories."

Sarah frowned. "Pa doesn't say much about the war, Leah. He gets a strange look in his eyes, and his jaw tightens whenever he's asked to tell us things. Even after all these years, he still has an occasional nightmare."

Deborah nodded. "My pa doesn't say much either, though sometimes, I hear him, Zeb, and Uncle Jonathan mention a battle or general when they're together and don't think anyone else is around. He has nightmares too, but Ma calms him down."

"Do you think Peter, Big Tom, Mammy Sue, or Elliot know anything, Leah?" Rachel frowned.

Leah turned to Betsy. "Grandma Edna said this woman showed up twenty-five years in the past?"

Betsy nodded.

Leah sounded as if she were simultaneously calculating dates and events as she spoke, "1857. Then the time period would exclude Elliot or Zeb unless someone told them about this mystery woman. Elliot came to help on the homestead after Uncle Jonathan left for war in '61. Zeb came home with him and Pa at the end of the war in '65. I'm guessing the others know something though.

"Peter was freed in '57 and traveled the trail with Grandma Edna, Grandpa Jim, Uncle Matt, Uncle Dwight, Aunt Josie, Annie, and Sean in 1858. His folks were freed before Ma, Pa, and Grandpa traveled the Oregon Trail after the war."

She rubbed her chin with a forefinger. "Grandpa Nate probably knew this woman, too, because he and our parents traveled together to Kansas Territory and claimed homesteads next to each other."

"Grandpa Nate." Deborah fidgeted. "Do you think he'll be ... all right, Leah? He'll be surrounded by a lot of people, and you know how grumpy he gets when his routine is upset. His memory seems to be slipping, too, and lately, he's been repeating himself."

"I'll keep an eye on him, Deb. If he appears to be getting too agitated, I'll get Pa or Uncle Jon."

A knock broke their concentration. "Girls?" Even through the solid door, Olivia sounded excited. "Are you ready? The last of our guests have arrived. We're waiting for you."

Betsy opened the door. "Come in, Livvy."

She stared, and moisture came and went from her eyes. "You all look so grown up. You're as pretty and bright as Christmas ornaments."

"You're beautiful, Mama." Rachel rushed to embrace Olivia, Sarah only a step behind.

Olivia hugged them. "We'd better go down. The men are trying to hide how hungry they are, but I can tell. They look toward the dining room every minute or two, and their noses twitch like hounds catching a scent."

Betsy's heart raced. They would enter the Aubry dining room with all eyes on them. Even though those who waited were mostly fathers, uncles, brothers, relatives, or friends, she felt like a debutante at her first ball.

When they stepped into the dining room, all conversations stopped. The males stood if they weren't already standing.

Betsy smiled at Matthew Bell. The astonished admiration so clearly showing in his blue eyes made all the hours she'd spent sewing her dress worth every moment.

He walked to her and held out his elbow. "May I escort you to your chair, Betsy?"

She nodded and placed her hand in the crook of his arm.

As Matthew slid her chair under the table, she glanced toward her friends. Her eyebrows raised when she watched her brother, Corbin, offer to escort Leah. The look in his eyes for her friend showed a depth of emotion she hadn't seen from him before. He shuttered his expression in a moment, but she'd seen.

Startled, she stared at the two. Corbin and Leah? Did Corbin care Leah was not quite two years his senior? She watched her brother. His athletic physique and serious face reminded her of Daddy Sean—a scholar with callouses. At sixteen, Corbin stood a head taller than Leah. The muscles of his shoulders stretched the fabric of his shirt, and his biceps corded under his sleeve when he moved her chair. His strong jaw showed no hint of childhood. He'd taken on a man's responsibility on their ranch at fourteen, so maybe the age difference didn't matter to him.

Betsy studied Leah's face from the corner of her eyes. How did her friend feel about her brother?

"You're staring."

At the sound of Matthew's deep voice, Betsy turned to him. "Everything and everyone is so pretty, tonight, don't you think? I want to remember this night forever."

He placed the napkin on his lap. "You're one of the prettiest."

Betsy looked around to make sure no one could hear her and then stared in Matthew's eyes. "So are you," she whispered.

His laugh came from deep within his belly.

"Shh." She frowned.

He lowered his voice. "Pretty? Me? Come on, Betsy, stop teasing."

"Beauty is in the eye of the beholder, Matthew Bell."

He laughed again. "Well, something must be in your eyes

then, but you can believe I'm pretty all you want. Just don't tell anybody. When you wake up from whatever Christmas dream you're in and see me in my soot-covered work clothes and with my hands dirty from swinging a blacksmith's hammer, don't blame me if you think I'm not so pretty. I warned you."

Betsy watched a couple of the neighbors' daughters bring around serving plates and begin to serve the guests.

Uncle Phineas had hired an extra cook and a few local women to help with the meals and housekeeping during the holidays, since the Bostonian relatives were staying at his ranch—The Aubry Rocking A—instead of at her house.

For this, Betsy was thankful. Their place was too small to house so many guests comfortably, and she didn't want to be around Grandfather when he asked her, for what seemed like the fiftieth time, when she was going to get married, or when was she coming to Boston to live.

Daddy Sean could only take so much of Grandfather, too, so the housing arrangements suited him as well.

Matthew dug into his food with enthusiasm, while she took small bites and savored the flavors.

He stared at her, his fork half-way to his mouth. He lowered the utensil. "You eat so daintily—like someone I knew a long time ago. She chewed every bite and never talked with food in her mouth. I'm sure we disgusted her by the way we ate."

Chills raised on Betsy's arm. Could this woman from long ago be the mystery woman? She took a deep breath to calm her suddenly racing heart.

"Really?" She glanced around as if she weren't totally involved in the conversation. "Why do you think the way you ate disgusted her?"

"For years, we smacked and spoke with food in our mouths. Sure has taken us awhile to lose these habits." Matthew looked toward Sean. "Thanks to your dad and my long-ago friend, Peter and I learned our manners. They were good models."

"I'm glad." Betsy sipped her soup, her mind spinning to try to find ways to keep him talking. "Daddy told us he taught you and Peter after your friend left."

Matthew nodded. His attention caught when he saw Annie, Josie, and Olivia laughing at some joke. His eyes took on a far away look.

"Why are you looking at Mother, my aunt, and cousin like that?"

He jerked and fingered a small scar near his jawline. "They remind me of someone I knew a long time ago."

The mystery woman.

Keep him talking, but don't mention the woman directly. "I never noticed your scar before, Matthew. What happened?"

He chuckled. "Oh, I couldn't outrun a buffalo stampede when I was seven."

"What? You must have been terrified. Tell me."

He shrugged. "This woman I knew saved me. She pulled me into a crack in the ground and covered me with her body as hundreds of the beasts crashed through the homestead."

Betsy gasped. "Did she get hurt?"

"Yes, a buffalo calf's hoof gashed her arm as she moved to protect me." His words slowed and quieted until they stopped altogether.

"Your mother said she missed her after all this time. Do you?"

He nodded and resumed eating.

Betsy searched his face. The closed expression in his eyes

told her the conversation about the mystery woman was at an end.

"Matthew? I'm glad she saved you. I'm glad you're here beside me."

He patted her hand. "I am too, Betsy."

CHAPTER TWO:

DIVIDE AND CONQUER

Leah Johnson
PARENTS: Jesse Johnson and Mary Bell Johnson
SIBLINGS: William, Zach, Deborah
UNCLE, AUNT, COUSINS: Jonathan, Olivia, Rachel, Sarah
UNCLE, AUNT, COUSINS: Dwight, Josie, Susana, Polly
UNCLE, GRANDPARENTS: Matthew, Edna, Jim Bell, Nate Johnson

"Will you sit at table with me, Leah?"

Corbin smiled, and I stared. When had Sean and Annie's son grown up without me noticing? A brief glimpse of something in his gray eyes gave me pause. The look came from the heart of a man, not a boy.

"Yes, I would be happy to."

He seated me then looked around. "Quite the spread. Our families haven't been together on this scale for awhile."

He eased into his chair and turned to look at me. "You're beautiful as always, Leah."

I eyed his freshly shaven face and his best Sunday-go-to-meeting shirt. "You dress up pretty nicely yourself, Cor."

His smile crinkled the corners of his eyes. "When I have to. Not much need to get fancy when most of my time is spent on the back of a horse or behind a pair of pliers and a roll of wire."

My interest sharpened. "Did you get the new horse pastures fenced before snow fell?"

"Yes, with David's help."

We glanced toward his younger brother. He sat next to his Bostonian Grandfather, his face flushed and his lips tight.

"Uh-oh. Grandfather must have said something to raise his hackles. Probably he suggested my brother leave the ranch and return to Boston with him so he can get a job doing real work."

I studied the West patriarch. "Really? Betsy said he urged her to come to Boston and find a wealthy man to marry."

Corbin turned his gaze on Sean and Benjamin. "No wonder my father and uncle homesteaded in Kansas for awhile. They left the family shipping industry to be their own men. I don't think Grandfather has given up hope yet Dad and Mom will move us all to Boston so we can live happily ever after in the West mansion with Uncle Ben, Aunt Laura, and Charles."

"Sounds like he wants to be around family."

He turned to me. "More like he wants family to be around him, but he also wants to build his own little shipping empire using his sons and grandsons to do this. His firm is already a giant in the industry, but he wants to grow even bigger. He invited me to come back with him and Uncle Benjamin when they leave here after the new year."

"Are you considering this, Cor?"

He stilled, and his serious eyes met and held mine. "No. Everything I want is right here." His soft tone and intent expression conveyed a message I could easily interpret.

Before I could say anything, he picked up his fork and took a bite. I did the same.

We ate in silence until Annie, Olivia, and Josie laughed at something Grandpa Nate said.

Corbin chuckled. "They've been so happy about this big Christmas shindig. They talk nonstop when they're together."

His words focused my attention on the three women. "What do they talk about?"

"They relive some of their early years when they grew up together or when Mom and Aunt Josie traveled the Oregon Trail."

"Do they ever tell you some of their stories?"

"They used to."

"They're so animated and young-looking when they smile like they are now. What stories make them laugh?" I held my breath then released the air as slowly as I could.

"Mother tells about how dependent she and Aunt Josie were on the Bell family after Betsy's father accidentally shot himself and died on the Trail.

"They also laugh about how everyone who traveled with the Bells reacted with shock when they first laid eyes on each other."

"Even your father?"

"Yes. The most shocked seemed to be Father, Dwight, Matthew, and your Uncle Jonathan."

I glanced at the men. All were strong and self-assured. "Does this reaction seem strange to you, Cor?"

"What do you mean?"

"Do any of them look as if they could be shocked by the looks of identical twins?"

He studied each of the men. "No. Their reactions don't seem to match what I know about them."

We ate in silence, watching the subjects of our conversation.

"Leah?"

At Corbin's serious tone, I turned toward him. "Yes?"

"Would you—"

Deborah waved at me from across the table and mouthed, "Leah. Grandpa."

I leaned forward to see the confused look in Grandpa Nate's eyes as he looked around. His confusion seemed to be worse at night, and the sounds of several people talking probably didn't lessen his discomfort.

"Cor, Grandpa Nate's not feeling well. I need to help him up to his room. Please excuse me."

"Of course. May I help?"

"Thanks, but I think I can manage. If he gets stubborn and too hard to handle, I'll wave at you, and you can get Pa."

He stood when I stood. "See you later, Leah."

I saw that something in his eyes again, but he quickly looked away.

"Grandpa?" I leaned close to his ear. "The noise from so many people talking is giving me a headache. Will you walk me to my room?"

"Leah?" He seemed to have a hard time focusing on my face. Finally, his eyes cleared. "Sure thing, sweet one."

Without a word to the others, he pushed his chair back and took my arm.

We walked slowly toward the stairs, and I glanced over my shoulder. Both Uncle Jon and Pa watched me, a question in their eyes.

I shook my head. I didn't need their help yet. Uncle Jon's lips tightened, and his jaw clenched. Pa said something, and the muscles in Jon's face relaxed.

As we climbed the stairs and walked the hall, I patted Grandpa's hand. "Isn't this nice, Grandpa Nate? Look out the window. Look at the snowflakes."

We watched the snow fall for several moments, before I drew him into his room. "Why don't you sit in the rocker while I turn down your sheets?"

He didn't argue, which told me how tired he was.

"Grandpa, will you tell me a story?"

"I don't know many stories, Leah."

"Well, tell me about homesteading in Kansas, or the Civil War, or your days on the Trail. Or tell me what most surprised you when you reached Oregon."

He chuckled. "Those stories would take more than one evening, Granddaughter."

"I'd like to hear them." I patted his hand. "Did you notice how Annie, Aunt Olivia, and Aunt Josie laughed together at the dinner table? They sounded so happy, I wanted to laugh along with them."

"They did? What were they laughing about?"

"Something you said to them when you saw them for the first time. Do you remember?"

My heart raced as Grandpa frowned. "I'm havin' a hard time remembering things these days, sweet one."

"No matter. Let's get you tucked in. Do you want me to have Pa or Uncle Jon help you get undressed?"

"I can undress myself. I'm not old and helpless yet."

Tiredness and crankiness flavored his words. "Turn your back until I tell you I'm ready."

When he told me I could turn around, I sat on the edge of the bed and stroked his calloused, still-strong hand.

He chuckled. "I used to rub your hand just like you're doin' mine when you weren't no more than two. Remember? You'd beg your Grandpa Jim and me to 'go 'orse,' so we'd take you to the horses. You'd sit on them until we brought you back to your ma so she could put you down for a nap. You didn't like naps, so you fussed. I'd sit by your little rocker and rub your hand 'til you went to sleep.

"Mary wasn't happy with us, 'cause we'd let you ride without your stockings or hat. Your skin turned as brown as a nut."

I laughed. "Really, Grandpa? Tell me more."

"The trail was long. We just about didn't make it." His words slowed and he fought sleep.

"Were you glad to get to Oregon, Grandpa?"

His eyes jerked open. "What? Oh, yes. Didn't think we would. Dangerous, you know. Thought we'd starve before we got here. Lucky for us, Jim and Dwight Bell and Sean West came in the nick of time with supplies. Didn't like West at first. Too cocky. Came from a rich family, you know?"

"Yes, I know. Did you like Olivia, Annie, and Josie when you first met them?"

He yawned. "Gave me a shock, they did. Looked too much like that trouble-making woman who stayed with your grandparents for a few months."

My heart pounded. "Was she really such a trouble-maker, Grandpa?"

"Oh, yes. She would've struck that Frank—somebody—with a hoe handle. I could see the way she held the handle and how she seemed to be calculatin' the distance between 'em. Shocked everyone who'd come to the meetin', I tell you. She was strong enough she'd have done him some damage."

He chuckled and yawned again. "I shouldn't have stopped her. Strange, pants-wearing trouble-maker she was, but I didn't like that man much either. Needed to be brought down a notch."

Grandpa scowled. "She had Jonathan turned inside out so he didn't know whether he was comin' or goin'. Never saw him so out of kilter. When she left suddenly, she made a hole in him the war only made bigger.

"That woman had Dwight and Sean tied up in knots too. Thought they'd fight a few times. Always tense when she was around. Glad she left. Didn't want her for a daughter-in-law anyway.

"Should've thought out my ultimatum a little better. Had she agreed, we'd have been fussin' from mornin' to night, day in and day out."

"What ultimatum, Grandpa?"

He didn't answer for several moments.

"Grandpa Nate? What ultimatum?" I whispered near his ear.

He finally answered. "Told her if she wanted to free Peter, she had to marry Jonathan that day while we had so many witnesses. I said that because Jon wanted her. Didn't want the other two to cut him out."

Shocked, I tried to organize my thoughts. They raced around in my brain like wild mustangs.

I thought Grandpa was asleep, but he continued speaking, his eyes closed, his tone exhausted. "That woman wouldn't back down for anything. Nothin' but trouble she was. Standin' up for slaves and goin' against ..."

His voice trailed to silence, and I clutched his hand. "Grandpa, did you say something about this woman when you first met Olivia, Annie, and Josie?"

"Yep." He sounded as if he had to pull the memory through a long canyon. His voice faded and his eyelids dropped. I leaned forward to hear his whispered words. "Told 'em I hoped they weren't as much trouble as that Lexie Logan. She was a firebrand. They told me they weren't ..."

In less than a minute, Grandpa snored. I pulled up his blankets and kissed his cheek. My head spun and excitement raced through my veins.

Just then, Pa and Uncle Jon opened the door and looked toward the bed.

I put my finger to my lips and joined them in the hallway. Gently, I closed the door.

"Is he all right, Leah?"

"Yes, Pa. Just tired."

"I hate seeing him this way, Jesse. He's always been so strong." Jonathan's pain roughened his voice and tightened his lips.

"I know, Jon. I know. Come on. Let's rejoin the party."

"I'm not much in the party mood now."

"You ought to make the effort. Phineas brought in musicians. He thought we'd enjoy dancing."

"You know I'm not a dancer."

"Then just hold Olivia in your arms and sway. I don't dance either, but Mary doesn't seem to mind."

Uncle Jonathan's eyes brightened. "All right."

I wanted to ask him about his relationship with Lexie Logan, but I knew now was not the time. I could see the tension in his body and the strained look in his eyes. If I asked, he'd probably snap at me and close up like I'd seen him do a time or two before when someone upset him.

We returned to the large dining room to see the furniture pushed against the walls and musicians tuning their instruments.

I put my hand on my uncle's battle-scarred hand. "Don't forget to ask me to dance too, Uncle Jon. I'll do the dancing for both of us."

He stared at me. "You're a good girl, Leah."

I stretched up to kiss his cheek. "And you're a good uncle. Don't forget."

The corner of his mouth curled up. "I won't, though I may have a hard time wading through your beaux."

I stepped back and looked in his face. "My beaux? What beaux?"

He tilted his head.

I turned to see both Corbin and Charles waiting respectfully for me to finish my conversation.

Uncle Jon kissed my forehead and whispered, "They are real men, Leah. I don't think you can do better."

Both men approached when Uncle Jon stepped away.

"How is your grandfather?" Corbin looked toward the stairs.

"He's sleeping now."

Charles smiled. "Corbin refused to let me have the first dance with you even though I'm his elder and should be shown more respect, Miss Leah, so I'm asking if you'll allow me the second?"

I laughed. "Of course."

"Oh, Father says for me to ask you to reserve the third dance for him."

"Your father?" I glanced toward Benjamin West. He lifted an eyebrow. I nodded.

I enjoyed both dance partners. Corbin didn't say much, but his clear gray eyes and warm, gentle touch did. Charles's eyes sparked with merriment, admiration, and interest. My heart warmed to both of them. *Oh, dear.*

Dr. Benjamin West stepped forward for the third dance. "Thank you for agreeing to dance with me, Leah. My goal is to partner every one of the females at this party before the night is over."

"I saw you with Betsy the first dance and Polly the second. Only four more dances to go if you're partnering only the single women. You'll have an additional five if you intend to dance with Laura, Olivia, Annie, Josie, and Ma."

"My feet already ache at the thought."

My mind still buzzed with all I'd learned from Grandpa. I looked at Benjamin West. He would have known Lexie Logan. "I don't mind sitting this one out if you want to watch instead."

"Ahh. This sounds good. You won't mind?"

"No."

We sipped hot chocolate and watched the dancers.

After several moments, I worked up my courage to see if I could learn new information from him. I kept my eyes on the dancers but asked, "Look how young Annie, Aunt Josie, and Aunt Olivia look. Aren't they pretty?"

He studied the women. "Yes, they don't seem to age quickly."

We continued to watch. I kept my tone nonchalant. "Of the three, which do you think looks most like Lexie Logan?"

"Olivia, of course. They could have been identical twins." He turned to me, and his eyes narrowed. "Who told you about Lexie Logan? I thought talk of her was taboo."

I shrugged. "Grandpa." Then I laughed. "He called her a firebrand."

Ben chuckled. "Well, you know your grandfather. I'm sure he would consider an outspoken woman like Lexie to be a trouble-maker. She stood up to him, and they often butted heads."

I turned to him. "Did you think she was a trouble-maker, Dr. Ben?

"No. I wouldn't call her a firebrand or a trouble maker. I thought she was an intelligent, educated, and gifted woman who would've made my brother the best wife he could've asked for. They had a lot in common."

The dance ended, and Benjamin stood. "Thank you for your time, Leah. A word to the wise? Lexie Logan is still a sore spot for most who knew her. Tread carefully."

I nodded, and he bowed and left.

Chapter Three:

The Mystery Woman Revealed

Betsy Taylor West
Parents: Sean West and Anne Taylor West
Siblings: Corbin and David
Uncle, Aunt, Grandfather, Cousin: Benjamin, Laura, William,
Charles

"Betsy, dance with me?" Matthew Bell stood in front of her, his hand outstretched, a grin on his face.

The slow dance. The last of the evening. She took his hand and moved close. His strong arms drew her closer. She wanted to rest her cheek on his broad chest, but she kept her head upright.

She raised her eyes. "This has been the best night ever, Matt."

"I'll see what you say in a couple of days when you open your gifts on Christmas morning."

"Gifts are fun, but this," she looked around at her favorite people, "is better than gifts. Don't you feel the sense of warmth and love in this room?"

He glanced around and then down at her. "I do."

She studied his face as they danced, wondering what she could say to get him to open up about the mystery woman.

"What's wrong, Betsy? Why are you looking at me the way you are? Do I have something on my face?"

She slipped her hand up to his jaw and traced the scar with a fingertip. "No. Your face is fine." *All of you is fine—from the top of your black head to the bottom of your booted feet, Matthew Bell.*

She returned her hand to his shoulder and rested her cheek on his chest. His heart rate increased, and she sighed. The questions could wait.

After the dance, Phineas stepped into the center of the room. "Please get comfortable. I have a surprise for you before you retire for the night."

He motioned toward a young woman who held a violin and bow in her hand. "I'd like to introduce you to Leandra Hall, a talented musician from back east who is visiting her folks nearby. She will close us out with one of my favorite hymns."

From the moment Leandra played the opening notes of "It is Well With My Soul," Betsy noted the immediate and striking reactions of Jim, Edna, Dwight, Mary, and Matthew. Even Sean and Jonathan straightened and stared. Matthew's face paled and he sucked in a breath. "Oh, no."

Before the violinist had finished the first verse, Edna sobbed into Jim's shoulder, Mary turned her face into Jesse's neck and wept, and Dwight clasped Josie's hand as if hanging on to reality. Dwight looked at Jonathan. Jonathan sat rigid next to Olivia. Betsy wondered what the look meant.

"What's wrong?" Betsy whispered.

Matt shrugged. "This will stir up memories best left undisturbed."

"Why are your mother and sister crying, Matt?"

Matthew didn't answer for several moments. "This song reminds them of my sister and brother who died from cholera many years ago. The sound of the violin reminds them of Pa Fergus, Pa's and Uncle Dwight's Pa, who loved the violin. He died on the Trail. Most of all, the skill with which this musician plays reminds them of ..."

"Of?"

He hesitated. "Of a woman we knew long ago." He continued to stare at the violinist as he spoke in a low-voiced whisper, "No one could play the violin or piano like—. She made music come alive. We would listen to her play for hours after chores were done. We still miss her. She sang and played this song, so the music reminds us of our losses. Hearing this song is like hearing her voice."

The mystery woman. Betsy searched the room for Leah. When their eyes met, Leah nodded but returned her attention to Jonathan.

Why did she stare at Jonathan, Daddy Sean, and her Uncle Dwight with such intensity? With such curiosity? Had she learned something about the mystery woman? Did the information directly involve them?

Betsy snuggled close to Matthew's side. His warm hand covered one of hers. She closed her eyes and let the haunting sound of the violin wash over her.

When the last notes ended, no one moved or said anything for several moments. They appeared to be waking out of a dream. Uncle Phineas clapped, and the others joined in.

Grandfather stood and clapped, and Betsy joined him. He smiled at her, and she returned his smile.

If only he'd keep this same good humor throughout his visit and would leave off trying to convince her to return to Boston with him, she'd enjoy his company more.

Then the men helped the musicians pack up their instruments and return the furniture to the correct rooms and positions. Uncle Phineas lit a lantern and led the male musicians to the bunkhouse and told them breakfast would be ready for them by seven so they could get an early start.

"Leah." Betsy signaled her friend to wait for her on the stairs. "You found out something, didn't you?"

Leah nodded. "I did, but I'm exhausted. Shall we talk tomorrow?"

Betsy nodded. "Come on. The other girls are probably undressed and in bed. They slipped away a little before the violinist finished playing."

In the bedroom they shared for the holidays, they helped each other undress by the light of a candle. Betsy glanced toward the cots full of sleeping cousins and placed the candle under a globe in case any had to get up in the middle of the night.

After she and Leah slipped under the down comforter, Leah turned toward her. "Have you ever wondered who our people really are?"

"What do you mean?"

"We only know one side of them—the parent or relative side. We don't know what kind of people they were twenty-five years ago."

Betsy stared. "I'd imagine they would be much the same. Why do you think they'd be different?"

"Something Grandpa Nate said tonight made me think Uncle Jon, Uncle Dwight, and your Pa were a lot less ... mellow ... than they are now."

Betsy paused to process the comment. "I watched you dance with Jonathan tonight. He seemed disturbed. Did you ask him about our mystery woman?"

Leah sighed. "Her name is Lexie Logan. No, I didn't ask because he was already upset. He hates seeing Grandpa getting old."

Betsy sat up. "Lexie Logan? How did you discover her name?"

"Grandpa Nate. Seems he didn't get along with her at all."

"All right, tell, Leah."

"Maybe I should wait until the others wake up. Then, I'll only have to tell the story once."

Betsy yawned and lay down. "You're right. I can barely keep my eyes open." She hesitated. "Leah, how do you feel about my brother?"

Several heartbeats passed before her friend answered. "I like and respect Cor, Betsy. He's not a boy anymore."

"You have a lot in common, you know? He's a hard worker and steady. He's smart too, like Daddy Sean. You aren't bothered by the age difference are you?"

Leah chuckled. "There's less than two years difference between us, Betsy, which is several years less than the seven between you and Uncle Matt."

"We're older now, Leah. Age doesn't seem to matter as much. Do you think your feelings for Corbin could grow into more than liking and respect? I know you saw the look he gave you, so you know his feelings have grown into love."

Leah whispered. "Yes, I saw. I don't know, Betsy. I'm not used to thinking of him as more than a friend. I need to get acquainted with the man he's become. Don't get me wrong. I have a great deal of affection for Cor, and I won't belittle his feelings for me."

"Good. Promise you'll give him a chance?"

"I promise."

Betsy turned on her back and locked her fingers behind her head. "Charles likes you too. What do you think of him?"

"I met your cousin only two weeks ago, Betsy. I don't know him well enough to say."

"Surely you have an idea."

Leah turned on her back. "He's charming, handsome, and amusing. He has the sophistication one would expect from someone who grew up in a large city in your grandfather's house and under Dr. Ben's and Laura's influence." She tilted her head and smiled. "Are you turning matchmaker, Betsy?"

"No. You're my best friend, and I'd like to keep you in my family. I'd prefer you as sister-in-law, but if you can't see your way clear to marrying Cor, then Charles is the next best thing."

Leah chuckled. "If you marry Uncle Matt, you'd be in my family. You'd be my aunt. Did you ever think of this?"

"Being your aunt sounds terrible, Leah. I am two years younger than you. I can't imagine calling you Niece."

"Don't be silly. You'd still call me Leah."

Betsy yawned. "Well, Matt hasn't asked me to marry him, so I don't have to worry about this for awhile. Goodnight. See you in the morning."

Betsy took pleasure in her friends' expectant faces as they clustered around her and Leah in her bedroom.

Rachel leaned forward. "All right. Tell. I know you and Leah discovered something."

"Leah found out her name, so I'll let her tell what she found out, and then, I'll tell you what I discovered."

Sarah stood. "Wait. I want to write the main points down so we can piece this puzzle together. Do you have paper, pen, and ink?"

Betsy pointed toward the small desk and waited for her to return. "You can use the breakfast tray as a writing surface."

Sarah placed the tray over her lap and dipped the pen in the ink. "Okay, I'm ready."

Leah told what she'd learned, and Betsy added her information.

Polly frowned. "Read the list, Sarah. This is making my head spin."

Sarah put the pen down, picked up the paper, and read.

1. Mystery woman's name = Lexie Logan.

2. Stayed with Jim, Edna, Dwight, and Matthew Bell for a few months. Dainty eater. They still miss her.

3. Saved Matthew from a buffalo stampede.

4. Jonathan, Jesse, Sean, Peter, and Benjamin all knew her. Jon, Dwight, and Sean loved her. Almost got in fights over her.

Sarah, Rachel, Polly, and Susana looked at each other, disbelief written clearly on their faces.

Polly frowned. "Sure doesn't sound like Sean. Can you see your pa being easily provoked into fighting over a woman, Betsy?"

Betsy shrugged. "Though he's strong, he wouldn't stand a chance fighting someone like Dwight and Jonathan. He'd most likely use words as weapons instead of his fists."

"Go on, Sarah, read the rest." Deborah leaned forward.

5. All were shocked when they saw Annie, Josie, and Olivia.

6. Olivia and Lexie could be identical twins.

"How could two unrelated women look like identical twins?" Rachel shook her head. "This doesn't make sense to me."

Betsy agreed. "But this explains why the men were shocked to see Olivia."

> 7. Nate called Lexie a trouble-maker and firebrand—she stood up for slaves, almost hit a man with a hoe handle.

> 8. Wore pants. Strong.

> 9. Nate gave her ultimatum: marry Jonathan to free Peter.

"I can't believe Pa would love such a strange woman." Rachel jumped to her feet and paced. She stopped in front of Leah. "Grandpa said he gave this ultimatum?"

Leah nodded, and Rachel continued to pace.

"Keep reading, Sarah." Deborah's soft voice refocused everyone's attention.

> 10. Talented musician: violin, piano

> 11. Benjamin said she was educated and intelligent—Sean's perfect match.

Betsy's throat tightened. How could a pants-wearing firebrand be Daddy Sean's perfect match?

No one spoke for several moments. Then Deborah stood and stretched. "So now we know answers to some of our questions, what questions still remain unanswered?"

Sarah answered first, "I want to know why this woman was so attractive to my pa. Though she may look like Mother's twin, Lexie Logan doesn't sound anything like Mother. Can you imagine my mom wearing pants, or planning to hit a man with a hoe handle?"

Betsy shook her head. "No. I want to know why Uncle Benjamin said Lexie was Daddy Sean's perfect match. I agree with Sarah. She doesn't sound anything like my mother except for the education and intelligence comments."

Polly grimaced. "I wish Grandma Edna and Grandpa Jim would be more forthcoming. Even Uncle Mattie. Don't they know the more they hide things from us, the more we want to uncover their secrets?"

Leah stood. "I wish Ma would open up. I want to know where Lexie Logan is, and what will happen if she shows up in our lives after twenty-five years."

Her comment silenced everyone and turned the mood more solemn.

A knock startled them. "Girls? Time for lunch."

Betsy opened the door. "Come in, Aunt Laura. We were just about to come down."

Laura looked around. "This looks like a serious meeting. Is everything all right?"

"Yes, everything's fine, Aunt."

Leah stood. "Laura, how long have you know my family—the Bell family?"

She smiled. "For quite a long time now. I met both the Bells and Johnsons at a box supper many years ago. Why?"

"Do you remember Lexie Logan?"

"Of course. She is a talented violinist." She chuckled. "Her music so inspired your great-grandfather Fergus, he decided to dance a jig with your mother with unpleasant consequences."

"How so?" Leah smiled.

"Fergus stepped on Mary's toes and brought them both to the ground. Fergus bumped his head in the process, and Ben gave him some medicine to ease his pain."

All the girls in the room leaned forward, barely breathing.

Leah laughed. "Ma never told me this story. I'll have to ask her to. Please, Laura, tell us more about the box supper."

She pursed her lips. "Well, the highlight of the supper was when Dwight, Sean, and Jonathan all bid for Lexie's box. The price got so high, all the other men dropped out of the bidding."

"Who got the box?" Deborah's voice reflected the intensity on all the other faces.

Laura laughed. "An older gentleman in his late eighties walked off with the prize. I had a hard time controlling my laughter when I saw the men's faces. I think Fergus put the man up to the bid."

Betsy grinned before her face turned serious. "Where is Lexie Logan now, Aunt Laura?"

"I'm not sure. Ben and I left for Boston before Sean went to Oregon with Leah's grandparents. I think Edna told me she returned to the States."

Betsy signaled, and all her friends rose and moved toward the door.

"Laura, one more question?" Leah stepped up beside her. "We all know Lexie looks a lot like Annie, Josie, and Olivia. Of the three, who would you say Lexie's personality and actions most resembles?"

"Hmm. Good question. From what I've seen and heard, she would be most like Josie in temperament."

"Ma?" Susana and Polly asked at the same time.

Laura smiled. "Yes."

Chapter Four:

Digging Deeper

Leah Johnson
Parents: Jesse Johnson and Mary Bell Johnson
Siblings: William, Zach, Deborah
Uncle, Aunt, Cousins: Jonathan, Olivia, Rachel, Sarah
Uncle, Aunt, Cousins: Dwight, Josie, Susana, Polly
Uncle, Grandparents: Matthew, Edna, Jim Bell, Nate Johnson

I dried the dishes Ma handed to me before giving them to Grandma to put away. I eyed Grandma Edna from under my lashes, then glanced at Ma. They worked companionably, and I could feel the love they had for each other.

I took a deep breath. Now was the time. "Ma, tell me about the box supper when you and great-grandpa Fergus tried to dance."

Grandma Edna laughed, and Ma tilted her head at me. "This happened many years ago, Leah."

"I know, but I'm sure you remember. Tell me, please."

Ma looked at Grandma Edna, a guarded look in her eyes. "Well, the music was so lively, Pa Fergus asked me to dance. He tried to hop from one foot to another and tripped us up. We ended on the ground in a heap. I was embarrassed and worried. Pa banged his head and stayed unconscious for a time."

"Tell me about the box supper. What did you put in your boxes? Did Uncle Matt bid? What about Uncle Dwight?"

Grandma Edna chuckled. "We put fried chicken, vegetables, and pie in our boxes and tied 'em up real purty. Your grandpa bought my box and Mattie ate with us. I brung extra for him. So did the other women with children."

"What about you, Ma. Who bought your box?"

"Your pa, of course."

"Mary gave Jesse a peek at the boxes beforehand, I'm sure."

"Ma!"

Grandma Edna winked. "I saw you, Mary. Then Jesse told Jonathan."

"Whose box did Uncle Jonathan buy?"

Both women stilled. Ma turned toward the sink. "He ended up with some blond woman who spoke German."

"What about Uncle Dwight? Did he buy the first box he bid on, or did he get into one of those bidding wars I hear about."

They didn't answer for several moments. Then Ma spoke, "Yes, he got in a bidding war. No, he didn't get the first box he bid on."

"Who bid against him? This sounds fun."

"Why so curious, Leah?" Grandma Edna lifted an eyebrow.

"Doesn't a box supper sound like a great idea for us and the neighbors in the summer?"

"I guess so." Ma returned to washing dishes.

"So who did Uncle Dwight get in a bidding war with, Ma?"

Grandma Edna put away another dish. "Jonathan and Sean."

"Really? How funny. Whose box were they bidding on?" *Uh-oh. Maybe I pushed them too far.*

Ma kept her head down and Grandma Edna frowned.

Ma spoke without looking up, "We had a friend stayin' with us. They bid on her box."

"Lucky girl."

"She didn't think so, Leah. She'd never been to a box supper, and she was scared about havin' to eat with the highest bidder."

I stared. "She was *afraid* to eat with Sean, Uncle Jonathan, or Uncle Dwight?"

This didn't sound like the woman Grandpa Nate described.

Grandma Edna nodded. "The men were pressin' her hard. She didn't want to commit to any of 'em."

"Why?"

"Because she had a man waitin' for her in the States. She loved him. What was his name, Mary?"

Ma whispered, "Lance. Lance Garrett."

My thoughts chased each other. "Where is your friend now, Ma?"

Silence. I didn't think Ma would answer. "Kansas, I suppose. Maybe Guatemala."

"Guatemala?" My eyes widened. "What would she do in Guatemala?"

"If she returned to Lance, they were goin' to work in an orphanage."

I digested this information. The pieces of the puzzle known as Lexie Logan didn't fit. "Do you think she'll come to visit?"

"Never." Grandma Edna spoke without hesitation. "We won't never see her this side of heaven."

Ma shook her head and a tear slipped from the corner of her eye.

Pa walked into the kitchen and stopped suddenly when he saw Ma brush at the tear. "Mary, what—?"

"She's okay, Jesse. Just rememberin' a friend from long ago."

Pa knew. I saw recognition in his eyes. He nodded and turned to me. "Corbin wants to know if you'd like to ride for a couple of hours. The sun is out and the snow isn't deep."

"I'd love to. I'll run upstairs and change into my riding gear. You'll let him know?"

"Yes. Take Deborah with you."

"All right, Pa." I'd prefer Deborah as a chaperon over any of my other cousins, because she said little and observed much. She also rode better than they did.

Corbin had already saddled and bridled our mounts. He handed us our reins. His eyes softened when they met mine, but he looked away first.

We mounted, and I rode between the two of them out the impressive entry gates.

I breathed in the cold air and looked into the winter blue sky. "Ah. A wonderful day to ride, Cor. Thanks for asking."

"I had to get out of the house for a while and onto a horse. Figured you would feel the same way. Thought we'd ride over and check on the mares and yearlings in the far canyon."

"Yes. Let's pick up the pace a little."

Cor nudged his gelding. Deb and I followed. The cold air chilled my nose and cheeks. My exhilaration grew the farther we rode. My hair came unpinned from bouncing around under my hat, but I pushed the tendrils out of my face with an impatient hand. I loved the touch of cold on my face, the tangy smell of pines and snow, and the warmth and life of the horse I rode.

As we approached the West's pastures, Corbin stood in his stirrups and frowned as he looked toward his herd. "Something's wrong." He heeled his gelding forward.

The horses milled at the end of the pasture, heads up, ears pricked, and bodies tense. Their nostrils flared as they looked toward the fence bordering the forest. They snorted and whinnied.

Corbin slid the rifle from his saddle holster and checked the loads.

I drew my rifle and did the same. "Bear, cougar, wolf, or something else?"

"I don't know, but not human. Not the way they're acting. I need to get closer. You and Deb stay here."

Our horses' heads went up, and their bodies tensed. They turned toward the forest too.

Cor dismounted and handed me his reins. His fingers touched mine before he turned away.

Clouds covered the sun and a cool breeze chilled any exposed skin. I turned up my coat collar and tucked the muffler in tighter.

"I don't like this, Leah. Something doesn't feel right." Deb watched Corbin soft-foot his way toward the horses then glanced into the sky and shivered. "Looks like more snow."

Cor climbed the pole fence and disappeared into the woods.

I don't know how long we waited until we heard a shot and a roar. Bear. An angry, hurt bear. My heart raced, and I tried to keep control of our spooked mounts.

When ten more minutes passed without any sight or sound of Corbin, I fidgeted. "Deb, I need to see what happened. If Cor wounded the bear, and the animal turned on him, he could be—"

"I know. Be careful, Leah."

I dismounted and moved as cautiously as I could, my rifle up and ready. When I got to the rail fence, I slid the rifle through the rungs and propped the barrel against a post before climbing over. With the weapon in my hands again, I glanced once more at the restive mares and headed toward the trees.

Before I'd taken five steps, I heard the unmistakable grunting and snarling of the wounded bear. The animal approached faster than I could retreat.

Fear tightened my grip on the rife, and I backed up until the fence braced me.

"Leah," Deborah screamed. "He's coming."

My heart pounded in my ears as I released the front safety. Then I eased my finger toward the back trigger.

The bear stopped at my sister's scream then roared and lumbered toward her.

"Leah! Watch out!" Corbin fired in the air, and the bear turned. "Deb, ride toward the mares. See if he'll turn to follow you."

The angry, short-sighted bear stood on his hind legs, sniffing, confused, and trying to decide what he should do.

I fired. He roared, dropped to all fours, and charged. I dropped the rifle and rolled under the fence just as he hit the top poles. The fence shook and two of the poles splintered as he crashed through. I rolled back under the bottom rail and grabbed the rifle, shaking as I chambered another round.

The bear snarled and came for me, saliva and blood dripping from his jaws.

Boom! Corbin shot, and the animal fell over and thrashed. In moments, he lay still.

"Don't move, Leah. He may not be dead." Corbin climbed the fence and approached, his face pale and his rifle pointed at the bear. He stood over him for several moments before poking the animal's paw with the toe of his boot. No response.

"What's a bear doing out at this time of year, Cor? Shouldn't he be sleeping?" Deborah frowned.

Corbin shrugged and pulled his hunting knife out of the scabbard. "If the food supply is abundant and the weather mild, sometimes they may come out for a bit."

He frowned and looked toward the horses. They now grazed without agitation. "This old boy thought to have fresh meat and went after one of the yearlings. Looks like the claw marks are a couple days old."

Deborah turned her horse toward the others. "Which one? I'll go get him so we can bring him back with us and fix his wounds."

"The sorrel with three white socks."

"I see him. I'll be back." She untied her lariat and turned toward the horses.

"Take him back to the house and send a couple of men to help with the butchering, will you, Deb?"

She waved but didn't turn.

Corbin tilted his head toward me. "Since you're already bloody, why not give me a hand?"

"Bloody?" I looked at my clothing and grimaced. "Well, these are ruined unless Ma knows how to get the stains out."

"When the bear came over the fence, you were rolling under him, remember?" He stepped closer and pulled a handkerchief out of his coat pocket. With tender movements, he turned my chin with one hand and wiped the blood droplets off my neck and cheek with the other.

I stood still and stared at him. My eyes traveled the contours of his strong jaw and firm lips before moving to his intelligent eyes. Our gazes locked, and I saw into his man's heart. A muscle in his cheek moved, and my pulse jumped and picked up speed. When he trailed his fingers along my cheek and lips, I had a hard time breathing.

"Such soft skin and lips." He closed his eyes. "Just as I imagined."

"Cor, how long have you felt—?"

One side of his mouth curled upward, and he stroked my cheek with the pad of his thumb. "For a long time. Ever since I was old enough to recognize the strength of your spirit, the extent of your kindness, and the depth of loyalty you have for those you love. These called to me."

His words did nothing to slow my heart. "I don't know what to say. You seemed to have changed from a child into a man overnight."

"I haven't been a boy for a while, Leah. Not since my voice changed, I started shaving, and Father and I became equal partners on the ranch." His gaze intensified. "How long before you start seeing me as a man?"

"My vision is clearing already, Cor, but my mind may take a bit longer to catch up."

"Then let me speed the process." He drew me into his arms and kissed me like I never thought to be kissed. I closed my eyes to stem the rush of dizziness and grasped him around the waist to steady myself.

When he lifted his head, I opened my eyes. He cupped my face and kissed me again before turning toward the bear.

Breathe, I told my lungs. They had a hard time obeying.

By the time Pa and Uncle Jonathan reached us, I was able to breathe normally as long as I didn't look at Corbin.

They bent over the bear, and Pa whistled. "At least seven hundred pounds. In the spring, he'd probably be eight. Good size for a black bear." He looked at me. "Are you sure you're all right, Leah?"

"Yes, Pa. Corbin put him down before he could get to me."

"Thanks, Cor." Pa gave him a head tip before they bent to remove the entrails.

I watched how easily all three men worked as a team, each predicting what the other needed without the use of words.

Soon, they'd loaded the bear on a pack mule, ready to be taken home for skinning and processing.

"Didn't expect to have fresh meat this winter." Uncle Jonathan wiped his hands on his soiled handkerchief. "Smoked bear sausage. Haven't had this in a while."

We mounted and headed toward home. Corbin rode beside me, and whenever our eyes met, heat crept into my cheeks, and I lowered my eyes.

Blushing? I never blushed. Corbin had certainly moved me out of my comfort zone. I had to get control of my emotions. Good thing Pa and Uncle Jonathan rode ahead of us.

"Tell us what happened." Pa turned up his collar as large snowflakes swirled around us.

Corbin recounted the story. He'd seen my actions from the woods, so I didn't have to add anything.

"Jon, let's water the animals at the creek. They have several more miles to go." Pa patted his gelding's neck.

Uncle Jon nodded and turned off the trail.

We dismounted and let the animals drink. Pa searched my face. "You're mighty quiet, Leah. Are you sure you're all right?"

"Yes, I'm fine. Just thinking about some things. I need to wash my hands and face."

"Here, Leah." Corbin handed me his handkerchief.

"Thanks." I dipped the kerchief in the cold water and dabbed at my face and hands. I glanced at Pa.

His eyes slid to Corbin and then back to me, sudden speculation growing in his face. "Did Cor—?"

Panic pulsed through me. I did not want Pa asking questions I was unwilling to answer. I had to create a diversion.

I looked toward my uncle. "Some questions have been preying on my mind Uncle Jon. Maybe you can answer them."

He frowned. "Me?"

"Yes. Why did you, Uncle Dwight, and Sean love Lexie Logan to distraction?"

Both Pa and Uncle Jon jerked.

Corbin's eyes widened.

Pa frowned. "Who told you about Lexie Logan?"

"Grandpa Nate."

Uncle Jon faced me, the muscles in his jaw working. "Don't go there, Leah. Some topics are best left in the past."

I straightened and looked in his eyes. "Why?"

He turned and mounted without saying anything.

I stared at his rigid back. "Does Aunt Olivia know how you felt about Lexie?"

He didn't answer. His jaw tightened and he booted his horse into a canter.

The rest of us mounted and followed.

Chapter Five:

A Startling Proposal

Betsy Taylor West
PARENTS: Sean West and Anne Taylor West
SIBLINGS: Corbin and David
UNCLE, AUNT, GRANDFATHER, COUSIN: Benjamin, Laura, William,
Charles

Someone knocked. Betsy waited to see if more knocks followed. They didn't. "Not Leah or Deborah."

She opened the door. "Cor, what are you doing here?"

He acknowledged the Johnson and Bell cousins before answering. "I came to ask you a question, Sis."

"What?"

"Who is Lexie Logan?"

Betsy gasped. "How did you find out about her?"

He looked from the other girls to his sister. "Obviously, you all have heard of this woman."

Everyone nodded.

Betsy pulled Corbin into the room before looking down the hall both ways and shutting the door. "How did you hear? We've been trying to solve the mystery of who Lexie is for days. We found out her name yesterday, thanks to Nate. Our folks are always so secretive and uncommunicative when they speak of her. They won't discuss her at all if we're anywhere in the vicinity."

He told of their encounter with the bear and the conversation at the creek. "Betsy, Jonathan and Jesse flinched like they'd been shot. What surprised me the most, though, was Leah's reference to our father loving this woman to distraction. Leah's words, not mine. What do you know about all this?"

Betsy signaled to Sarah. "Get the list and read to Cor what we know about Lexie Logan. I think we need to add a couple more details."

Sarah read the items on the list then frowned. "I don't like hearing about Pa's reaction to Lexie's name. This makes me wonder if he still harbors feelings for her."

"How do you think Corbin and I feel learning our father may feel the same way?" Betsy glanced at her brother.

"I don't like their responses any more than you do, Sarah, especially if my Pa loved her to such a degree as well." Polly's eyes widened. "Laura said Lexie and Mother have similar personalities. Do you suppose he thinks of this woman every time he looks at Mother?"

Dismay sharpened Susana's voice. "Don't say such a thing, Polly. Now we've stirred up a hornet's nest. We know Lexie looks like our mother, Aunt Annie, and Olivia. Are we going to wonder if our fathers think of this Lexie woman every time they look at our mothers or aunt?"

Betsy turned to Corbin. "Will you help us? The more minds on this investigation, the better."

Corbin frowned. "I agree with Susana. I think you've opened a Pandora's box. Why would you continue searching? What if you find out the men in our family still harbor strong feelings for her? Then what? Will you tell our mothers? To what purpose? Won't your actions cause them pain?"

The coded knock sounded. Betsy opened the door for Leah and Deborah.

Leah's breath caught when she saw Corbin. Her brother stilled then his lip curled in his small, one-sided grin. Interesting. Betsy looked from one to the other before catching her two friends up on the conversation.

"What do you think, Deb? Should we continue our search for answers?" Betsy waited for her friend to consider. She often wished Deb would answer quickly, but fast wasn't her way.

"I think we should continue the search but should not share what we discover with our mothers or aunts."

Betsy looked toward Leah, who seemed distracted. "Leah?"

Her friend startled. When she spoke, her words sounded as if she dragged them from one place to another, "I agree with Deb. For my own comfort, I need to find out if Lexie is a danger to our happiness. Grandma Edna said she'd never come back and Ma agreed, but what if she does? Since the Transcontinental Railroad crosses the continent, she wouldn't have a hard time getting here."

"I never thought of this." Sarah stood and paced. "Do you think any of them have tried to contact Lexie since she left?"

Rachel shook her head. "Doubtful. Do you think they would since all of them seem so determined to keep knowledge of her hidden?"

Polly frowned. "What I want to know is what's wrong with Lexie Logan? Something doesn't seem right about her. What other factor than her looks, dress, and talent would put such a muzzle on their words?"

Susana's face paled. "Grandma Edna said she probably married her sweetheart and went to Guatemala. But what if her sweetheart died in the war and she never left the States? Aunt Mary said she could be living in Kansas. With the railroad making travel so much cheaper and shorter, she could come at any time."

"Whoa, there, Susana. She isn't coming today." Corbin chuckled and stepped forward.

Betsy pretended not to notice when he stopped next to Leah, his hand only a fraction of an inch from hers.

Cor continued, "This is all conjecture. Why would this woman travel to Oregon in the winter, without an invitation, to see people who may or may not welcome her? Besides, why would she suddenly show up after twenty-five years? She's probably dead. Though Oregon is far from Kansas, we do have a postal system. We receive Grandfather's letters from Boston regularly, so why wouldn't she write if she were alive?"

"How do we know she hasn't written to one of them? They wouldn't tell." Betsy tapped her lips with a forefinger.

"Even if she had, don't you think Jon, Dwight, and Father would have told her of their marriages?"

Betsy nodded. "I suppose she might stay away if she knew they'd married other women. I would."

Sarah stopped pacing. "Do you think Peter might talk? He and his folks are invited for luncheon."

Deborah straightened her skirt. "If you can keep him and Uncle Mattie away from each other long enough to ask the questions, you might get answers. If they didn't have different skin colors, you might think they were brothers."

Betsy straightened. "I think I might be able to keep Matt's attention long enough for one of you to ask questions." She looked at Leah. "I think you should talk to Peter. You're family is closer to him than any other."

"All right. I'll try."

Betsy's amusement grew. Corbin and Leah stood next to each other without touching or acknowledging the other's presence, yet Leah's lowered lashes and distracted look, and Corbin's stillness and posture indicated they were intently aware of each other.

"If we can get only two pieces of information out of Peter before Uncle Mattie takes him off hunting, what do we want to know the most?" Sarah sat at the desk and pulled a piece of paper and pen toward her.

They discussed possibilities for several minutes before Polly lifted her head and sniffed. "Dinner. I'm starving. Let's eat."

The younger girls stood, straightened their skirts, and walked toward the door.

Betsy turned back. "I'll be down in a second. I need to get my ..." She glanced over her shoulder in time to see Cor caress Leah's wrist and hand with his index finger and thumb. Leah stilled then turned her hand so his thumb stroked her palm. She clasped his fingers for a moment then released them and left the room.

"Wait, Cor." Betsy grabbed her handkerchief and moved toward the door.

Her brother turned back. "Sis?"

"What's happened between you and Leah? I could feel the sparks across the room. I saw you stroke her hand a moment ago, and she didn't reject you."

51

He looked as if he considered each word before speaking.

Betsy spoke before he could, "You kissed her, didn't you?"

He hesitated then answered in a soft voice, "I kissed her, Bets. I kissed her well. She will no longer mistake me for a boy." He offered his elbow. "Now let's eat."

Betsy eyed Grandfather West from the corners of her eyes. His jolly mood and jovial conversation raised her suspicions. Why was he so happy? Overt happiness seemed so out of character.

She looked across the table at Corbin. He shrugged and shook his head, so she turn to Charles, who sat beside her, and spoke in a low voice, "What's going on with Grandfather?"

Her cousin stilled and lowered his eyes. He fumbled with his napkin.

"You know something, don't you? Tell me, Charles."

He spoke near her ear, "Bets, give Grandfather a chance, please. He truly does want the best for all of us."

Betsy stiffened. "What does he want?"

"You know."

"For me to go to Boston. I've already told him no. What makes him think he knows what's best for me anyway? I've only seen him a few times in my life." She slid her gaze to Matthew, who sat next to Corbin.

"Wait until you hear his proposal, okay?"

"How do you know about this?"

Charles shrugged. "I wasn't exactly listening at the keyhole, but I overheard, Grandfather, Mother and

Father, Sean and Annie, and Mary and Jesse discussing the possibility of you and Leah returning to Boston with us for a visit."

Betsy stared. "They want Leah to come too?"

"Don't be angry, Bets. Grandfather thought you'd be more willing to come if you had a friend along. He wants to show you the places he loves."

"Why?"

Charles glanced at his father and grandfather. "I don't know exactly, but I think his wishes have something to do with his health. You know, Grandfather isn't young anymore."

Betsy stared at her grandfather. He looked perfectly healthy to her. She returned her attention to Charles. "What did Mary and Jesse say about Leah leaving?"

"Jesse seemed more resistant to the idea, but Mary wanted her to go."

"*Mary* did? Really?"

"She thought getting Leah away from the horses, cattle, and ranch hands would do her good."

"I hope Mary uses a more subtle and convincing approach. Her rationale is sure to raise Leah's hackles. Her answer will be a resounding no."

Charles smiled and glanced at Leah. "This is where Mother and Annie come in. They will be the ones to urge her to come after Grandfather asks her. Father will add his invitation. All Mary has to do is agree. I hope your friend decides to come. She will add sparkle and zest to our lives. She's so calm and assured, but she also exudes life and quick action. She energizes me just by being in the same room with her."

Betsy's eyes widened. "You really like her?"

Charles met her gaze. "Yes, I really like her. If you say no to Grandfather's proposal, Bets, I won't have a chance to get to know Leah better."

Betsy glanced at her brother, who sat on the other side of Matt next to Leah. She couldn't understand their low-voiced conversation, but she recognized the earnestness in Cor's tone. How could she consent to Grandfather's proposal when Leah's agreement to come with her would cause Corbin pain?

"I don't know, Charles. I'll have to think about this."

"Well, think fast. Grandfather just nodded to Mother and Annie. That's their signal."

Betsy's thoughts whirled. What would she say? Did she want to travel back with her relatives after the new year? Knowing Leah might come if she said yes weakened her resolve. They would have so much fun together. Charles was an added bonus.

She turned her gaze on Matthew. He was the only reason she hadn't accepted Grandfather's invitation. She couldn't figure him out. His actions and tone of voice showed he liked her, but did he love her as she loved him? Did he think she was too young to get married? She would be eighteen in a handful of months. What could be his reason?

Did he intend to ask her to marry him, or was she to remain his—what? The man was twenty-four, for goodness sake, and she wasn't getting any younger. He hadn't shown an interest in any other woman, so if he had some hazy plans of asking her to be his wife in the future, how long did he expect her to wait for him?

Her jaw firmed, and she whispered, "I have half a mind to take a cattle prod to you Matthew Bell."

Grandfather West cleared his throat and looked at each

person. "This has been one of the most enjoyable holidays I've had for a long time. Phineas, thank you for your hospitality. If you ever return to Boston for a visit, I would be honored to have you as a guest in my home."

Phineas nodded. "If I ever return, I'll take you up on your offer, William. Thank you."

Grandfather looked around the table. "The invitation goes for all of you." He paused and his voice softened. "Leah? Betsy? I'd like to extend a special invitation for you both to come back with us and stay until spring. We'll show you a good time. I promise."

Betsy understood the stunned look in Leah's eyes. Had Charles not warned her of Grandfather's intentions, she might have worn the same expression.

"Oh, please, consider William's invitation, girls. I'd love to have you around. We're short on women in the West home."

The sincere warmth in her Aunt Laura's voice further weakened Betsy's resolve.

Benjamin held out his hands to both of the girls. "Laura is right. You would brighten our days. Charles can introduce you to his friends, so you'd have other young people around."

Charles leaned forward. "Please come."

No one spoke for several moments. Both Matthew and Corbin looked as if someone had planked them across the head. Betsy brightened inside. Maybe absence would make their hearts grow fonder. Leaving might not be such a bad idea.

Leah frowned and looked from William to Betsy and then at her folks.

Betsy hoped Jesse's still form and expressionless face didn't signal his dislike of the idea.

Leah shifted in her chair. "Thank you, Mr. West, but I don't think—"

"No need to answer tonight, my dear. You and Betsy talk this over. Will you promise you'll give this invitation serious thought?"

Betsy nodded and looked at Leah. Leah agreed.

"You will make this old man very happy if you decide to come."

Nathan Johnson made a sound between a growl and a sigh. "My girl has no business travelin' to the other side of the continent in winter, William. What are you thinkin'?"

Grandfather West put his napkin beside his plate. "Don't worry, Nate. From Oregon, we'll sail to Sacramento, and then we'll travel the rest of the way via railroad. I've made arrangements with both the Central and Union Railroads. We'll travel in comfort in my private car. The trip is tedious, but shouldn't be dangerous. Winter has been mild so far. We had no trouble getting here."

"Doesn't mean you won't have trouble goin' back. Snow can pile up mighty high between California and Boston." Nathan pushed back from the table. "I'm tired. Think I'll go to my room. Goodnight."

Leah nodded to Betsy then stood and linked her arm with Nate's. "Come on, Grandpa. I'm going upstairs too."

Betsy's heart fluttered at the thought of being trapped in a Rocky Mountain blizzard or stranded on the plains waiting for someone to dig them out. Maybe traveling at this time of year wasn't such a good idea after all.

Horrifying stories of the Donner Party who'd been trapped in the Sierra Nevada mountain range almost forty years ago, intruded on her thoughts. Snow. Starvation. Cannibalism. She shuddered. The Transcontinental Railroad went through Donner Pass on the route east.

Charles touched her hand. "Don't let him scare you,

Bets. Grandfather has contacts with the Smithsonian Meteorological people as well as the Signal Corps and the Weather Bureau. We wouldn't have traveled here if he thought we'd be stranded along the way. As dry as the weather's been, we're more likely to encounter dust storms than snow. The dust has been bad all year and across several states."

Betsy frowned. "Make sure Grandfather has enough food, water, and shovels before we leave here, Charles."

Her cousin laughed. "Sounds like you've decided to come. Just make sure Leah comes with you, Bets."

CHAPTER SIX:

HEARTSICK

Leah Johnson
PARENTS: Jesse Johnson and Mary Bell Johnson
SIBLINGS: William, Zach, Deborah
UNCLE, AUNT, COUSINS: Jonathan, Olivia, Rachel, Sarah
UNCLE, AUNT, COUSINS: Dwight, Josie, Susana, Polly
UNCLE, GRANDPARENTS: Matthew, Edna, Jim Bell, Nate Johnson

As we climbed the stairs, Grandpa Nate warned me of all the dangers I might encounter if I traveled at this time of year. "That Transcontinental Railroad follows most of the same route we took comin' here, sweet one. I know how dangerous some of that country can be."

"Tell me more about your trip, Grandpa. What do you remember most about traveling the Oregon Trail?"

He patted my hand. "The tribes didn't want us passin' through their lands. They'd taken to attacking smaller trains, so your ma came up with an idea to make them think we had more guns than we did. The boys built and painted a wooden gun made to look like the Gatlin' guns the North used in the Civil War. Seemed to work. We weren't attacked."

"Ma came up with the idea?" I tried to picture my quiet, peace-loving mother generating such an idea.

Grandpa chuckled. "Don't sell you mama short, sweet one. She's quite spunky when pushed. Did I tell you about the time one of the men on the wagon train attacked her and me? Good thing your pa and Uncle Jonathan taught her how to use that knife of hers."

He pointed to the back of his head. "You see this scar?"

I touched the faint line. "Yes."

"That coward callin' himself a man knocked me out cold with a limb. I woke up just as your ma slashed his arm and disabled him."

"Ma, successfully defended herself with a knife? *Ma?*"

He laughed. "Yes, sweet one. And she can shoot as well as she can cut, believe me. You ought to ask her to show you her knife. She wears the same one in a holster on her right thigh. All she's got to do is slip her hand into a special pocket and pull the weapon out."

I shook my head to clear the amazement from my brain. "Why would she still wear a knife, Grandpa?"

"For the same reason your pa and uncle carry weapons with them where ever they go. Once you've been forced to fight, you're always aware, always ready."

He frowned. "Mary and I had us a rough go early on before you were born. Did she tell you this?"

"No, Grandpa. Tell me."

His frown deepened. "When she and your pa first met, she was a shy, obedient girl. Then that woman came to live with her. Mary was never the same after. I blame her for all the trouble your ma and I had. Sometimes, your ma would straighten and firm her jaw against me, just like—"

"Lexie Logan?"

He grumbled. "She taught your ma to look in the Bible for answers. That woman's anti-slavery sentiments rubbed off on her and her folks." He grimaced. "Even Jesse and Jonathan came 'round to her way of thinkin'. Changed everything, she did. Only stayed three months, but her influence stretches through the years."

Thoughts danced and spun in my mind. "Even today, Grandpa?"

He yawned. "Yes, sweet one."

I turned away so he could undress then sat beside him and stroked his hand.

His eyelids drooped.

"Grandpa Nate," I leaned near his ear. "Why did Lexie stay with Ma and her folks?"

Nate's eyelids fluttered. "Had no choice. The Bells found her sleepin' like a baby in the middle of the prairie. She had no idea how she got there. She was the strangest woman I ever laid eyes on."

"What?"

He patted my hand. "Better go and join the rest, sweet one. I'm too sleepy to talk now."

I kissed his cheek and rose. "Goodnight, Grandpa."

He snored as I left the room and closed the door.

Pa and Uncle Jon met me at the top of the stairs.

"How is he, Leah?" Uncle Jon glanced toward the door.

"Fine." I looked at Pa. "Does Ma wear a knife strapped to her thigh?"

Uncle Jon's eyebrows lifted. "She still wears the knife?"

Pa nodded. "Your grandpa told you?"

"Yes, he told me a lot of things." I looked from him to Uncle Jon and back. "What he told me makes me wonder if I know you or Ma at all. Even you, Uncle Jon."

His eyes narrowed. "What do you mean?"

I took a deep breath and let the air out slowly. "Why do you all shroud the past in mystery?"

He didn't speak for several heartbeats. When he did, his voice roughened. "Lexie. You're still digging for information about her, aren't you? Why won't you let the topic rest?"

"Because I'm scared."

"What?" Uncle Jonathan frowned. "Why?"

"I'll tell you if you'll first answer a question."

"What do you want to know?"

"Why did you love Lexie Logan?"

Uncle Jon's nostrils flared and his jaw tightened. He remained silent so long, I thought he wouldn't answer.

His words came out rough. "Because she made me feel alive. My blood sang whenever she stood close or challenged me, which she did every time I saw her. She resisted my advances, which only made me want her more. I enjoyed the chase even more, because I knew Sean and Dwight loved her too."

He flinched. "Every time I smell vanilla, I think of her."

The knot in my gut tensed. "You still love her, don't you? What about Aunt Olivia?"

"Lexie is Lexie, and Olivia is Olivia. Though they look alike, they are two different people. I love Olivia more than my own life."

"What if Lexie comes here, Uncle Jon? This is what I'm afraid of."

His eyes softened. "She will never return, Leah. Put your fear to rest."

I shared the cousins' conjectures about Lexie. Both Pa and Jon shook their heads.

Pa stroked my cheek. "We will never see Lexie again until we get to heaven."

"How do you know? How can you be so sure? Is she dead?"

Jon's eyes met Pa's. Pa shook his head.

Uncle Jon tapped my nose with his index finger. "Lexie will never return. Have no fear."

Their assurances frightened me even more. How could they say with certainty she would never return unless—

"What's wrong, Leah? You're pale. Are you going to faint?" Pa reached for me.

I stepped back and took a deep breath. "I'm okay, Pa. I just need some air."

They followed me down the stairs. I stopped them before I stepped outside. "I'm okay. I'll be in soon."

Both nodded and turned. Uncle Jon glanced over his shoulder before he closed the door.

The bile climbed into my mouth, and I bent over the porch railing and vomited. How could they be so certain Lexie would never return unless they had made sure?

No! The people I loved were not murderers.

The door opened and Betsy spoke, "Leah, are you all right? Jesse sent me out here to check on you."

She stopped next to me, concern furrowing her brows. "You're sick?"

"Yes." *Heartsick.*

She put an arm around my shoulders. "Let's get you cleaned up and into bed."

When my cousins and Betsy returned an hour later, I pretended to be asleep. I waited until their whispers tapered into deep breathing before I slipped from under the covers and grabbed the blanket at the end of the bed.

I crept down the stairs. Several of the single men slept nearby, so I tiptoed to the door and turned the handle as slowly as I could. I eased myself through and settled in the porch swing.

As I rocked, I remembered Grandma Edna's assurance Lexie would never return. I'd seen Ma's tears and her agreement. Now Pa and Jonathan both insisted she would never return. Each had spoken with a tone of certainty.

The more I tried to explain their certainty, the more uncertain I became, and the faster I pushed the swing.

"Leah? Are you okay?" Though Corbin whispered my name, I could not mistake his voice. I stopped the swing.

"I'm ... not okay, Cor. I couldn't sleep for thinking."

He eased himself on the seat next to me and buttoned his coat. "What's wrong?"

"I can't voice my concerns. They sound ridiculous even when I think them."

"But they disturb you, nonetheless." He pulled on his gloves.

"Yes," I whispered and drew the blanket tighter around me. "Will you do me a favor, Cor?"

"I'll try."

"Ask Sean if Lexie Logan will ever return."

"Sounds easy enough."

"If he says no, ask him how he knows? My guess is he won't give you a straight answer."

Corbin moved closer to see my face. "This is about Lexie Logan and not about Grandfather's invitation?"

Before I could answer, the door opened and closed behind Charles. He whispered as he pulled on his coat and gloves. "A midnight tryst in the dead of winter sounds delightful. I'm game. Don't hog the swing, you two. Move over."

Cor and I shifted to the right and made room for Charles on my left. The heat from both men cocooned me in sudden warmth.

"Ah, nice and comfy. Who came up with this brilliant idea?"

"I suppose I did. I came out here to think."

He nodded. "Thinking is good, especially if you're thinking about saying yes to Grandfather."

"Don't be so pushy, Charles." Corbin stiffened beside me.

"Other thoughts held my attention, I'm sorry to say."

"Sorry?" Charles peered at me. He frowned. "You do look worried. What's wrong?"

"I'd rather not say."

"All right. Let's say nothing. We'll just swing."

I don't know how long we sat without speaking. The quietness and gentle movement lulled me into a more relaxed state. I closed my eyes. Corbin moved closer. Charles rested his right arm on the seat behind me and did the same.

The grandfather clock in the hall chimed two o'clock. Corbin moved, and I sat up. "We'd better get back inside. I don't relish facing an angry Jesse Johnson."

We stood and tiptoed to the door.

"You first, Charles." Cor pointed. "Make sure we're clear."

"You'd better be right behind me, Cousin."

We entered quickly, and I climbed the stairs without stepping on a creaky board. I slipped into the bedroom and slid under the covers.

Betsy turned toward me and whispered, "Are you okay?"

"Better. Do me a favor?"

"Of course. What?"

"Ask Uncle Matt if Lexie Logan will ever return. If he says no, ask him how he knows. I'm sure he won't give you much of an answer, but tell me his exact words, okay?"

She yawned. "Okay. Don't forget Peter and his folks are coming for Christmas Day luncheon tomorrow—today. I'll try to keep Matthew occupied so you can talk to Peter. Give me a wink when you're ready. Just don't wake me too early."

Ma looked in the mirror and straightened her skirt.

"Will you show me your knife, Ma?"

Her eyes widened. "Who told you I wore one?"

"Grandpa Nate. He says you're good with the weapon. He says you're skilled with a rifle and pistol too."

"Your pa and uncle made sure I was. We lived in dangerous times. Your grandpa talks too much. Did he give you all the details of the attack? He told everyone who'd listen for years after."

"No, just generalities. Why didn't you tell me about the attack?"

"Because the memory is painful, Leah. Though the man intended rape and murder, I maimed him. Don't know if he lost his arm and eventually his life because I cut him. I did the best I could to sew him up, but I'm no doctor."

"The knife?"

Ma reached into her skirt and pulled out a knife with a wicked-looking blade. She held the weapon with great familiarity.

"Why do you still wear this? The attack happened a long time ago."

"Bad dreams come every now and again. The knife makes me feel safer, more in control."

"You're the most in-control person I know, Ma."

"Looks can be deceivin', Leah. I'm often fearful and, like the next person, live with regrets." She turned and unclasped the necklace she'd worn since I could remember. "Here, turn around. I have a Christmas present for you."

We stood side-by-side and looked at the diamond heart necklace now hanging from my neck.

"The necklace is beautiful, Ma. Did Pa give this to you?"

Ma didn't answer for several seconds. When she did, tears choked her words. "No, a very special woman gave this to me on my sixteenth birthday."

My eyes met hers in the mirror. "Lexie Logan?"

She closed her eyes and nodded. "Lexie."

So many questions swirled in my brain, I didn't know which one to ask first.

She opened her eyes. "Well, enough of the past. Let's head down to lunch. Peter, Mammy Sue, and Big Tom should be here by now."

I followed her to the door. "You loved Lexie, didn't you, Ma?"

Ma nodded. "She was like a sister to me and Mattie. Though she was often in pain and afraid, she gave of herself. Spent hours teachin' Mattie and Peter to read."

"She taught Peter to read?"

Ma nodded.

"Even though the laws at the time made this a crime?"

"Yes."

The mental image I had of the woman called Lexie Logan continued to shift with each new piece of information. Against my will, I liked our mystery woman.

Before we descended the stairs, I caught Ma's hand. "Why was she afraid? Did Sean, Uncle Dwight, and Uncle Jon scare her?"

Ma didn't speak for several moments. When she did, her words were so soft, I had to lean closer. "She wasn't afraid of the men. She was scared she'd never see her loved ones again. She didn't know how to get home."

"Ma,—?"

"Hush now, Leah. We're sittin' down to eat."

"Leah?"

I looked up at my name. Charles pulled out a chair for me. "Sit by me?"

"Where's Cor?" I glanced around.

"He's in the barn showing Grandfather his horse." His cherubic look raised my suspicions. Had he put his grandfather up to getting Corbin out of the house for a few minutes?

"All right."

He slid my chair in, sat, then studied my face. "You're still worried about something, aren't you?"

"Yes."

"Don't be upset with me, Leah, but I'd like to suggest a trip to Boston may give you respite from your worries for a time."

His suggestion caught and held my attention. Would three months away give me time to clarify my thoughts?

"You don't want to live with regrets, do you, Leah? If you don't come, you'll always wonder what you missed."

Regrets? Ma said she lived with regrets. Were her regrets tied to Lexie Logan? Did she wish she hadn't done something, or she had?

I looked at her for several moments before returning my attention to Charles. "All right. If your Grandfather desires my company so much, then I'll be happy to accompany Betsy to Boston."

I looked toward the door as Corbin and William entered. They were in time to hear Charles's jubilant words, "Leah's coming, Bets, so pack your suitcases."

CHAPTER SEVEN:

SLOW AS MOLASSES

Betsy Taylor West
PARENTS: Sean West and Anne Taylor West
SIBLINGS: Corbin and David
UNCLE, AUNT, GRANDFATHER, COUSIN: Benjamin, Laura, William,
Charles

Betsy nodded when Leah signaled for her to keep Matthew's attention. She watched as Peter followed her friend outside then stood. "I think we should talk, Matt."

He pushed back his chair and rose. His strained expression indicated he might have something to say as well. "Fetch your coat, Betsy. I'll meet you outside."

Betsy hurried to her room and put on her warm coat, knitted hat, and muffler. She called to her mother as she rushed down the stairs, "I won't be gone long. Don't let them open presents without me."

Matt paced the porch. The look on his face made the blood rush through Betsy's veins and heat flood her cheeks. She didn't know whether to be scared or excited. She chose the latter.

"Come." He pointed toward the corral.

His stride was so long, she had to take two steps to his one to keep up.

When they reached the back side of the corral, the side farthest from the house, Matt swung around and faced her. He crammed his fists in his coat pockets. "Why are you leaving, Betsy?"

She cocked an eyebrow. "Why shouldn't I? Grandfather invited me."

"I heard him talking to Benjamin and Laura. He wants you to find a rich husband while you're there. Said he wants more grandchildren." Matt's lips thinned to a hard line. "Is this what you want?"

"I don't know about *rich*, but I'm open to the idea of a husband and children."

Matthew's jaw flexed. "I always supposed—"

Betsy stood tall. "What did you suppose?"

"You and I ..." His nostrils flared and he bit down on his words.

Betsy stared at him for several moments. "What am I to you, Matthew Bell? A friend? A sweetheart? What? I've never been able to figure this out. You've never let on what's in your heart."

In one fluid motion, Matt removed his hands from his pockets and pulled Betsy into his arms. His kisses sent fire through her.

He lifted his head and kissed her forehead. "Now you know what's in my heart. I'm the man for you, Betsy. Not some easterner who may want to marry you for your connections."

"Why haven't you said anything to me before?"

"I wanted to make sure I had a comfortable place for you—for us. For the last two years, I've been building a home. Bought the land and started building. The house is almost finished." He took a step back. "Do you love me?"

Betsy flung her arms around his neck and drew his face down to hers.

He pulled her closer.

She traced the contours of his jaw with a finger. "Yes, I love you."

He reached in his pocket and drew out a small box. "I've wanted to give this to you for a long time."

Betsy opened the box. Her eyes widened at the sight of two diamond rings—a wedding band set—and the breath left her lungs.

"Assuming your folks will give us permission, will you marry me Betsy West?"

"Yes. When?"

Matthew laughed. "In the spring, after you return from Boston. I'll have everything ready for you by then."

"Boston? You still want me to go?"

"As long as you're wearing my engagement ring, I think you should. You'll have fun, and you can keep an eye on Leah. I've been watching her. Something's not right. Do you know what's bothering her?"

Betsy stepped back and nodded. "I do, but I'm not sure you're ready to hear what this is."

He stared, then rubbed his jaw. "Lexie."

"Yes."

He sighed and pocketed the rings. "I wish I could tell her more, but I can't. All of us who knew Lexie well made promises. I must keep mine."

"Can you at least tell me if Lexie might return? This disturbs Leah the most. She's afraid Dwight, Daddy Sean, and Jonathan still have feelings for her. She doesn't want her aunts and cousins to be hurt."

"Lexie will never return." Matthew's tone held no doubt.

"How do you know?" Betsy searched his face.

"I just know."

"Is she ... dead?" Besty's throat constricted around the word.

"No, she hasn't—never mind. When do you want me to ask your folks for permission to marry you?"

Charmed by his words, Betsy shoved Lexie Logan to the back of her mind. "Today. Now."

Matthew twined his fingers with hers. "Then let's go back to the house."

When she could do so without anyone seeing, Betsy spread her fingers and moved her hand so the diamond engagement ring glittered. She placed her hand on her lap, covering the ring with her other hand.

"You look like the cat who swallowed the cream, Sis. Why?" Corbin sat next to her on the sofa as they waited to open presents.

"I'll show you, if you won't say anything to anyone. They'll find out soon enough."

He nodded, and she spread the fingers of her left hand.

"Engaged? Matt?"

"Yes."

He looked up and met the amused eyes of Matthew Bell who watched him from a chair near the Christmas tree.

Matt cocked an eyebrow.

He looked at his sister. "I don't know what to say. Does this mean you'll not return with Grandfather?"

"No, I'm going. I intend to buy some things for our wedding and for the house Matthew is building us."

"So Leah is leaving too?"

"Yes." Betsy searched his face. "Why don't you come with us?"

"To tag along like a love-sick puppy? No thanks. I love Leah, but if she needs space, I'll give this to her."

"You're not afraid of Charles winning her affections?"

Corbin didn't speak for several heartbeats. "I don't enjoy the thought of them living in the same house for three months, but I know Leah well enough to believe Charles won't turn her head."

Olivia, Annie, Josie, and Edna distributed gifts, and the noise level rose as people laughed and wondered what was in each wrapped package.

Like a child, Betsy tingled with anticipation. The colors, smells, sights, and sounds of the Christmas season enchanted her, but no material gifts could compare with those of being with friends and family. Love swelled her heart as she looked around the room. Her eyes met Matthew's. His clear blue eyes sparkled and happiness split his face.

She returned the sentiment.

"Betsy? Here's a gift for you." Olivia handed her a rectangular box tied with a dark blue ribbon.

"Thanks, Livvy." She waited until all the others had their gifts and, when Jim Bell whistled, they all tore the wrappings to see what was inside.

The laughter and thank yous raised the noise level even more. Betsy opened her box to see a string of costly pearls. She looked at the card and then at her grandfather.

He smiled and nodded.

She rose and hugged him. "Thank you, Grandfather, they're beautiful."

He caught sight of her ring and sobered. "What's this, Betsy?"

Everyone sitting nearby looked up as William captured her hand and lifted her fingers to the light.

The Bell and Johnson cousins gasped.

Leah mouthed, "Auntie."

William frowned and looked around the room. "Who?"

Matthew stood and approached, and Betsy's heart raced. This giant of a man would soon be her husband.

He removed Betsy's hand from William's, kissed her ring finger, and intertwined his fingers with hers. "Me, sir."

"Sit down, young man. I don't like people to tower over me." He turned to Sean and Annie. "You approve of this engagement?"

"Yes, Father." Sean and Annie nodded.

All the girls swarmed around Betsy and Matt. They oohed and aahed over the diamond and teased Matthew about being as slow as molasses.

Nate chuckled. "No use frettin' yourself, William. We've seen this comin' for a while."

Betsy laughed, then sat down next to Matt. She watched the others show off their gifts, but kept a careful ear on her grandfather's conversation.

William grunted. "I had plans ..."

"Well, you know what they say about the best laid plans. Which reminds me—hope you don't have plans for Leah."

William's gaze met Nathan's. "What do you mean?"

"I mean Leah isn't easily driven. She can be as stubborn as a mule if she feels you're tryin' to push her into somethin' she doesn't want to do. Just givin' you a heads up."

Betsy agreed, though she didn't say so. She looked toward Leah. Her friend's head was bent close to Corbin's and the look on her face as she listened to him disturbed Betsy.

What did they talk about? Leah's face reflected an emotion Betsy had never seen her wear before. Did fear shine from her eyes, or was the expression uncertainty?

Betsy intended to find out once the excitement settled.

An hour later, Nathan stood and yawned. "Think I'll talk to the sandman."

Betsy giggled at her grandfather's puzzled frown. She picked up torn wrapping paper and whispered, "This is Nate's way of saying he's going upstairs to take a nap."

Not long after, the others drifted away. All said they needed to get home and take care of livestock. Only Nate and Leah remained.

The Bell and Johnson cousins said their goodbyes with good-natured teasing and hugs. Betsy laughed and promised she'd see them soon, but breathed her relief when only Leah remained to share her room.

"Grandfather? If you don't mind, I'm going to go to my bedroom. Thank you for the pearls."

He chuckled. "Maybe I'll talk to the same sandman. Don't tell anybody though. My reputation for being awake on all counts might be ruined if word got out." He scanned the room. "Looks like Benjamin and Laura must be meeting with the same busy gentleman."

When Betsy entered the bedroom and shut the door, Leah turned from gazing out the window.

"What's wrong, Leah? What did Corbin tell you? I've never seen that look in your eyes before. Come on, tell."

"I asked him to get the same information from Sean as I asked you to get from Uncle Matt. Were you successful?"

Betsy nodded. "He said Lexie Logan will never return. He couldn't tell me why, because he and the others who knew Lexie well made promises not to talk about her."

"Peter told me the same thing." She lowered her voice. "I'm worried, Betsy. The only reason I can think of as to why they are all so sure is they were involved with her disappearance."

Betsy paled. "Do you realize what you're saying?"

Leah nodded. "I can't believe any of the people I love are murderers, but I can't figure out any other way they can be so certain they will never see her again. Can you?"

"No, but I'm sure they didn't harm her. I asked Matt if she was dead and he said—" she frowned.

"He said what?"

"Hmm. He said no, she *hasn't* and stopped his next words instead of saying she *isn't* or *wasn't*. Strange. What do you suppose he intended to say?"

Leah stared. "I don't know, but he absolutely said no?"

"Yes."

"That makes me feel better, but they are still hiding something important. Something they don't want anyone to know."

Betsy stretched. "Let's talk of something happier, like our trip to Boston, or me becoming your aunt in three months."

Leah made a face. "I'm not sure the trip is a happier topic. I don't have the kind of clothes I'm sure your Grandfather expects me to wear, and I don't know anything of eastern ways."

"Don't worry, Aunt Laura will teach us what we need to know. Grandfather will probably buy us dresses."

Leah stiffened. "Absolutely not. I won't be beholden to your grandfather for my clothes. I've saved money, so I'll buy what I need within reason. I don't want to get too many things I can't use when I return."

Betsy pointed up. "Uncle Phineas said we should go up to the attic and check out the luggage situation. Shall we?"

"I suppose."

They entered the attic and stared at the jumbled heaps of miscellaneous objects.

"Whew, this place needs a good dusting." Betsy put her hands on her hips and looked around.

Leah smiled and her expression lightened. "Just like the attics in ghost stories. Intriguing."

They cleared a path to a stack of trunks. Betsy pulled several carpetbags from the pile and examined each piece. "These will work even though they're old fashioned. What do you think?"

"Fine with me. What do you think is in the trunks, Betsy?"

"I don't know. Let's find out."

They pulled a couple of trunks into the middle of the room. The lids opened without keys.

Leah's eyes shone. She pulled out a journal and read the title. "Look, Betsy, Olivia's journal. This one is dated 1858."

"And here are journals Daddy Sean and Aunt Josie wrote the same year." A couple of letters fell from the pages. "Letters to and from Mary and Matthew."

"Let's take these to our room and read them in comfort. I want to know what happened to Lexie Logan. Maybe they will mention her."

Back in the bedroom, Leah opened Olivia's diary and scanned the pages. "Listen to this, Betsy." She read.

I've read their diaries and begged for their stories so many times they wonder why I want to hear them again. I wrote down everything they told me in another diary, so I can go back and relive their experiences with them. I've also been allowed to make copies of the letters sent between the Bells and Mary, and Peter and his folks.

Lexie seems to be a paragon of virtues, from what Edna, Jim, Dwight, Mattie, and Sean tell me. All of them admire her musical ability, which must be great, because they tell me she can make the violin strings and piano keys sing with joy, sadness, fear, and anger like no one else. Her playing gave great joy and comfort to Fergus before he died, and touched even the hearts of a Kansa brave.

Though none of them talk about Lexie very much, they do let a few things drop. Sean talks about her education, Edna comments about her need to be clean, and Dwight mentions her strength. Mattie told Josie Lexie always smelled like vanilla and could run faster than anybody he knew except maybe Washunga and Allegawaho. Edna told Josie these were the sons of the Kansa Indian who responded so well to her music.

We couldn't imagine how any woman could run faster than men or children in the kind of shoes, or long, bulky skirts we wear, but Edna said she wore men's pants and a shirt that fit her curves. Edna blushed when she said this. Josie was shocked and asked if Lexie was a moral person. Edna said, "the moralist." She said getting used to Lexie took a while, but she was glad she could finally see beyond her clothes to the woman underneath.

Josie asked why Lexie ran, and Edna said she ran mostly to relieve the heartache of being away from her family and sweetheart.

Betsy frowned. "So what happened to Lexie Logan?"

CHAPTER EIGHT:

THE PAST SPEAKS

Leah Johnson
PARENTS: Jesse Johnson and Mary Bell Johnson
SIBLINGS: William, Zach, Deborah
UNCLE, AUNT, COUSINS: Jonathan, Olivia, Rachel, Sarah
UNCLE, AUNT, COUSINS: Dwight, Josie, Susana, Polly
UNCLE, GRANDPARENTS: Matthew, Edna, Jim Bell, Nate Johnson

I reached for a letter written from Sean West to Ma dated August 31, 1858, Oregon. I reread the last paragraph several times. "Listen to this, Betsy. Sean wrote to Ma to tell her about Great-grandpa Fergus's death."

Edna wanted to remind you of the hope Lexie gave us all before she left. Within the next ten or more years, the Transcontinental Railroad will be built, and we will be able to see each other again. She prays you will not lose hope.

Betsy's eyes widened. "What do you suppose he meant?"

I stared at the text. "Doesn't sound like Lexie left with hard feelings. She gave them hope they would be reunited by the Transcontinental Railroad." I looked up and frowned. "How could she know about the Railroad?"

Lexie Logan truly disturbed my peace.

We read quietly for several more minutes before Betsy yelped. I looked up from the letters. "What's wrong?"

She stared at me with wide eyes and colorless cheeks. "Listen to your mother's letter to your father while he fought in the war."

March 15, 1864, Kansas territory

Dearest Jesse,

I miss you so! I pray for your health and safety every day, and for an end to this war so you'll come home to us. The news in the papers is never good, but at least your name and Jonathan's hasn't showed up in the hundreds of dead, wounded, missing, or captured. I count down the days on the calendar to the date Lexie said General Lee would surrender at Appomattox Court House, and though the end is thirteen more months away, these months seem like years.

She gazed at me with wide eyes and colorless cheeks. "Lexie Logan knew when the war would end? She knew the date and place General Lee surrendered? How, Leah? How could she know such things unless—"

I had trouble breathing. "Unless what?"

Betsy whispered, "Unless she has supernatural knowledge. Is this possible, Leah? She seems to be able to predict the future with total accuracy."

"I don't know. We know she is intelligent, even Benjamin admits this. Maybe she has contacts high up in the government who tell her things?"

Betsy frowned. "Even if Lexie could move in such elevated ranks, which I doubt because of the description of her clothing, do you think these contacts would know when and where Lee would surrender? That they could know more than a year into the future? This doesn't make sense. Could they know the Transcontinental Railroad would be built more than ten years before the event? I suppose her contacts would know about the Railroad, because building one takes planning and time to raise money, but the surrender at Appomattox Court House?" She shook her head. "I'm scared, Leah. What if she's—"

I waited, but she didn't continue. "What if she's what?"

Betsy leaned toward me and whispered, "What if she's an angel?"

"Do you think an angel would come as a woman dressed in men's pants? I don't see examples in the Bible of God sending anyone looking like this to interact with humans."

"Then maybe she's ... not from God?"

My mind whirled. "The Bible says the evil one, like a thief, has come to deceive and destroy. Nothing I've learned about Lexie matches.

"She taught Peter and Uncle Matt to read and write regardless of what others thought. She stood up for Peter against Grandpa Nate. Her music touched the hearts of Great-grandpa Fergus and a Kansa warrior.

"Uncle Jonathan, your father, and Uncle Dwight love her. Ma, Grandma Edna, and Uncle Matt love and miss her. Didn't Grandma Edna say she was glad she got to know Lexie? Doesn't this say something about her character? She acts like a woman—like a human. Besides, Grandpa Jim loves God and his word so much, he'd never be taken in by a demon."

Betsy rubbed her temples. "I don't know what to think, Leah, but the mystery has only deepened. What should we do now?"

"Let's read the diaries and letters through from beginning to end in the order they were written. Maybe we missed something."

Betsy stood and stretched. "All right, but not until tomorrow. I'm too tired now. All this mystery has given me a headache. I'm going to go down and talk to my brother and cousin. Are you coming?"

"Yes, let me wash my face and hands first."

When we entered the living room, Corbin, Charles, and William West sat around a table and spoke in low, interested voices as they poured over papers and ledgers filled with columns of numbers. They pushed these away and stood when Betsy and I entered.

Their admiring gazes made me glad I'd washed my face.

William smiled. "Well, my day just got brighter. Boys, get our ladies chairs. They can join us."

Corbin and Charles obeyed.

Cor moved my chair next to his, and Charles seated Betsy between him and William.

William looked around. "Cozy."

I scanned the papers. "What are you doing?"

Corbin hesitated and looked from Charles to his grandfather. "Discussing business."

"Business?" Betsy laughed. "I thought you came all the way from Boston to get away from business, Grandfather."

"May I ask what kind of business?" I looked at the men.

William nodded. "I'm pleased you asked. We're talking about joining together in a new venture. If successful, this will secure my grandsons' futures and that of their families for some time."

My heart picked up speed. For the last few years, I'd considered ways I could earn more money to buy land.

Now that the law allowed a single woman to own property and conduct business as a sole trader, I had my eyes on a hundred and sixty acres of forest and grassland near a clear running stream.

I yearned to see my own horses and cattle grazing near a comfortable, well-built home.

Two problems stymied my dreams though. I had to be twenty-one, and I had to have enough money.

I sighed. I wouldn't be eighteen until spring. A few more years to go and a lot more money to earn.

What I earned from training and selling horses didn't add up quickly enough. At this rate, I'd be in my dotage before I could buy the land, so William's words caught and held my attention. He knew business, so who better to ask advice from than a giant in the business world?

"I've been thinking about a venture of my own, Mr. West."

At my words, all three of the men stared at me as if I'd grown extra heads.

Betsy's eyes danced when she noted their shocked expressions.

"Business?" William cleared his throat and looked at me. He smiled. "You're a woman, Missy. Women don't have heads for business, or numbers, or the ability to deal effectively with—."

"Uh-oh. Wrong thing to say, Grandfather." Betsy shook her head and looked from him to me.

Without a word, I reached across the table and pulled a ledger toward me and ran my fingers down the columns of numbers.

I then studied the contents of some of the letters and looked up. "You're considering teaming up with ice producers to provide ice for domestic use, since commercial sales have dropped. The company you're looking at has a world-wide market, and you're considering the cost of transportation by ship and rail."

William gaped.

I delighted in his astonishment. "Your son, Sean, taught my cousins and me, along with Betsy, Cor, and David for many years, Mr. West. I worked hard to make him proud." I closed and handed the ledger to him. "Oh, by the way, you have an addition error in the first column of the second page."

Betsy laughed until tears streamed. "I wish I had a photograph of your faces. Priceless."

William frowned and opened the ledger to the second page. His lips pressed into a thin line, then he snapped the ledger closed.

Corbin's brows furrowed. "What business venture, Leah?"

I shared my dream with them. My words quickened as I tried to paint a picture of the house, the green pastures, and the sleek, well-fed horses.

No one said anything after I finished. Charles stared as if I were a new species of woman, but Corbin masked his expression.

William drummed his fingers on the table and gazed at me for several long moments. "I don't know what to say, Miss Leah."

"Can we start over? Now that I've shown I understand business and numbers, I'd like to ask for your advice on how I can earn enough money to be able to buy the property when I turn twenty-one."

He glanced from Corbin and Charles to me. "Wouldn't you prefer to marry and leave such business to your husband?"

My eyebrows lifted. "No, why would I? I've handled horses and ranch business for many years. Pa started me young. I'm not afraid of hard work, and the men of my family will help me build if I ask them, so I think I'll be successful."

"You don't say anything about wanting a husband and children. Do these fit into your plans anytime soon?"

I didn't look at anyone except William. "Of course, I expect to have a husband and family, Mr. West. I just don't know when."

"What if you find someone or something you want in Boston? Would this change your plans?"

I smiled. "Everything I want is here, Mr. West."

Corbin's sharp intake of breath signaled he understood my words.

William rose, and the rest of us stood. "Let me think about your request, Leah. If you have some money to invest, I think I may know of a couple of opportunities you might be interested in."

My heart pounded as I walked through the door behind William, Charles, and Betsy. I could almost see my name on the land patent. I wanted to shout and dance.

"Did you mean what I think you meant, Leah?" Corbin's soft words near my ear stopped me.

I turned my head to see his face only inches from mine. "Yes."

His eyes shone. "We need to talk soon. Meet me at the porch swing after dinner?"

"All right."

He stepped to my side and clasped my hand. "Grandfather wants me to come to Boston with him. He wants me to check out business opportunities with Charles. I've talked things over with Father and Mother, and they are in agreement. You won't mind if I come, will you?"

"Of course not, Cor."

He chuckled. "You may not, but I'm sure Charles will. He planned to have you to himself for three months."

After dinner, Grandpa Nate and William established themselves around a chess board. I knew they'd be there for awhile. Betsy had gone upstairs to read, and Charles had mentioned catching up with his correspondence.

I smiled at Cor and tilted my head toward the porch.

He put on his hat and coat and slipped out the door.

I did the same, grabbing a blanket from the sofa before going outside.

"Look at the stars." Corbin stood at the railing and stared into the sky. "I never get tired of seeing them."

I joined him. The winter air chilled my nose and cheeks, and my breath turned white when I spoke. "Let's sit."

He sat close and wrapped the blanket around us. He pushed the swing a few times with a booted heel. "Where do we start, Leah?"

"Where do you want to start?

He turned my face toward his. "I love you. Do you love me?"

"Yes. Your kiss jolted me into evaluating what I really felt about you."

"The stick-together-through-thick-and-thin kind of love?"

"Yes."

"The I'll-still-love-you-when-you're-wrinkled-and-gray kind?"

"Yes."

His eyes glistened in the moonlight and he stroked my cheek with the back of his fingers. "Good. I love you the same way. Now that we are agreed, where do we go now?"

"Boston?"

He chuckled. "Yes, where I'll buy your ring. Then?"

"I don't know, Cor. Assuming your grandfather can help, I'm hoping to have enough money to buy that land in a few years." I thought about possibilities. "Do you think he will take my proposal seriously?"

"Business proposals are always serious to him."

He relaxed against the cushions and gave the swing another push. "Tell me about this piece of land. Does the property have other water sources? Natural boundaries? Lumber for building?"

I couldn't control my excitement. Words gushed from my mouth.

"Describe the land adjacent to this piece." He listened and asked detailed questions. "I'd like to see the place. Maybe we can ride out there soon if the weather holds."

"What's in your mind, Cor?"

"I'm interested in grazing land too. If the place looks good, I could file for a hundred and sixty acres next to yours when I'm old enough."

"If we married, we'd have three hundred and twenty acres." The concept took my breath away.

He intertwined our fingers. "Not *if*, Leah. When."

"I wonder what our folks will say?"

"They'll say we should wait until we turn twenty-one, file on our places, and then get married."

"I suppose that makes the most sense given the way the property laws are written." I leaned my head against his shoulder. "Seems like a long time to wait."

"Yes, to me too." He lifted my left hand. "Would you mind a long engagement? I want to get my ring on your finger as soon as possible."

"You'll have to talk to Ma and Pa first."

"I will. They're coming for lunch tomorrow, so I'll ask after the food has mellowed them."

I laughed. "Mellow? Pa? He doesn't have a mellow bone in his body."

Cor's lip curled. "I know. I've been around Jesse Johnson all my life."

"What about Sean and Annie? When will you tell them?"

"In the morning, after they get here. Dwight, Josie, Olivia, Jonathan, and all the cousins will be here, too, so I need to talk to them early before the noise level gets too high."

Sean, Dwight, Jonathan. My thoughts returned to the diaries and letters. "Cor, Betsy and I found journals and letters our folks wrote to each other. The earliest were dated 1858."

He stopped the swing. "Did they mention Lexie Logan?"

"Yes, even Sean. They are hiding information about her. She knew the events of the future many years before the future happened."

"What?"

I told him what we found and what we suspected. "Do you think she could be ... supernatural, Cor?"

He shrugged and booted the swing into motion. "I don't know. Even if she is, she hasn't been in their lives for twenty-five years."

I snuggled the blanket around me. "Of the people who knew Lexie well, who do you think might be the most likely to talk once Betsy and I show them the diaries?"

"I don't think you'll be successful if you approach the men one at a time. They've made promises. Maybe you and Betsy should get them and your mother in a room with you tomorrow, lock the door, and show them the diaries and letters."

My thoughts whirled. "I'll talk to Betsy tonight. We need to determine our approach."

"Wish I could join you, but I'll keep Charles, Father, and Mother occupied when you give me the signal."

CHAPTER NINE:

A SHOCKING DISCOVERY

Betsy Taylor West
PARENTS: Sean West and Anne Taylor West
SIBLINGS: Corbin and David
UNCLE, AUNT, GRANDFATHER, COUSIN: Benjamin, Laura, William,
Charles

Betsy looked up when Leah walked in. Journals and letters surrounded her on the bed.

Leah yawned and stretched. "Did you find anything?"

"No, but I got more insight into our folks' personalities."

Leah unbuttoned the buttons at her wrists. "What about Lexie?"

"Not much more, though I get the sense her presence permeated their thinking and actions in the months and years that followed her departure."

"When and how did she leave?" Leah unpinned her hair and let the long tresses tumble around her shoulders.

Betsy frowned. "I don't know. I didn't see anything in the journals or letters. Didn't Nate say something about her leaving suddenly?"

Leah picked up a brush and met Betsy's eyes in the mirror. "Yes. He said her sudden departure left a hole in Uncle Jonathan the war only made bigger."

Betsy laid down one of the letters. "You look—glowing. Where have you been?"

"Out on the porch swing. In the cold. With Cor." Leah turned and brushed at a tangle. "He's coming to Boston with us."

"And?"

"We're getting married."

Betsy squealed and launched herself from the bed into Leah's arms. "I'm so glad. When?"

"In a few years. We have to be twenty-one to claim land. This will give us time to save for the things we need. We'll talk to our folks tomorrow." Leah looked toward the bed. "Tonight, we need to come up with a plan of action to get your pa, Uncle Jonathan, Uncle Dwight, and Ma to talk about Lexie Logan. Cor thought we should get them all together and confront them with the journals and letters."

"Do you think they'll tell?"

Leah shrugged. "I don't know. Here, let me help you clear the bed off. I'm tired."

"Give me a few minutes." She grabbed her toothbrush and nightgown and opened the door.

When she returned, she stopped in the doorway and stared. "What's wrong, Leah? Why are you so pale?"

Leah looked at her with wide eyes. "Close the door. Look." She held out the diamond heart necklace her mother had given her and pointed to the inscription on the back.

Betsy brought the lamp closer. "Lexie Logan. Happy twenty-second birthday. Love, Mom and Dad."

"Look at the date," Leah whispered.

"*2014!*" Betsy stared and held the necklace closer to the light. She had not misread the numbers. "Lexie Logan visited from more than a hundred and fifty years ago? How is this possible, Leah?"

"I don't know." She rubbed her temples. "But this explains why none of our people want to talk about her around others. Who would believe their story if they told the truth?"

Betsy frowned. "They would probably lose credibility and business. People would think they were unstable or untrustworthy. I think I'd assume this if I heard such a story."

Leah hooked the necklace around her neck. "What I still don't understand is why she showed up when she did? Why did she leave so suddenly, and how did she leave? Did she return to the future? And why does she look so much like Aunt Olivia, Josie, and your mother? Coincidence? I don't think so. Maybe—?"

Betsy stared. "What?"

Leah fingered the necklace. "Do you think the reason Lexie looks so much like Livvy, Josie, and Annie is because she is one of their descendants?"

"A descendant?" Betsy's jaw dropped. "The idea boggles my imagination."

"I wish we could communicate with her somehow."

"How? She hasn't been—" Betsy straightened. "That's what Matthew intended to say when I asked if she was dead. He said no, 'she hasn't—.' The only words that makes sense are *been born*."

Leah stared at the necklace. "This stayed in the past with Ma. Maybe we could pass this to our daughters or nieces with the instructions to pass this on to their daughters. We could send a note."

"Do you know through how many generations the necklace would have to travel?"

Leah nodded. "Don't remind me. I'll be long dead before Lexie would ever get her necklace."

"This conversation depresses me. We're just starting to live. I don't want to talk about dying." Betsy blew out the lamp.

"Then think about how we're going to confront our folks."

"All right, Leah. I'll sleep on this. Goodnight."

Betsy's eyes followed Mary, Jesse, Mother, and Daddy Sean as Leah and Corbin led them into the sitting room and closed the door. She hoped the answer to Cor's proposal would be yes.

"Why do you look so satisfied with yourself, Bets?" Charles slipped into the chair beside her.

"I expect to hear good news soon."

He looked toward the door. "Good news? Tell. I could use some good news."

Betsy lowered her lashes and her voice softened. "You probably won't think what I have to say is good, Charles."

He sat back and looked from the door to her. "Tell."

"Leah and Cor have agreed to marry. They're getting the folks' permission now."

Charles's countenance fell. "I suspected as much. No matter how much effort I expend to engage her attention, her eyes always stray to Cor's. His do the same. I get more undivided attention from her cousin, Rachel."

"What's this? Who's getting married?" William slid into the chair next to Charles and laid several sheets of paper on the table in front of him.

"Shh, Grandfather." Betsy looked toward the door and then at him. "Leah and Corbin."

"What? I thought Leah wanted to invest?"

"She does. They won't marry until they turn twenty-one, because they want to file on adjoining pieces of property. They'll each be sole traders, and Leah's land will be filed in her name, not in Cor's. They intend to save as much money as they can to start the building projects as soon as they have the land patents."

Grandfather said nothing for several moments. He shuffled the papers in front of him and finally looked up. "This speaks well of them. They have self-control and self-discipline, and they don't seem to be in a rush or afraid of hard work. Just what they'll need as investors."

Betsy fidgeted. "What is taking them so long?" She watched the hands on the grandfather clock as they passed the thirty minutes mark.

She drummed her fingers on the table until William placed his hand over hers. "Patience is a virtue, Granddaughter."

The door opened and Mother, Daddy Sean, Mary, and Jesse stepped into the room.

Betsy studied their faces. Mary looked resigned, but Jesse and her parents smiled. Then Leah and Cor came out holding hands, and Betsy's heart pumped joy through her veins. She and Leah would be legally family twice over.

Grandfather waved the two over and signaled them to sit. "I understand congratulations are in order?"

Leah and Corbin nodded and sat.

Daddy Sean raised an eyebrow.

Grandfather waved him away.

He followed Mother into the other room where the noise level indicated many prepared for lunch.

"I've thought over your request, Leah, and I have a few options for you to consider."

Leah leaned forward, her eyes shining. "Yes?"

"What's your preference? Iron and steel works, rubber and rubber products, ready-made clothing, coal and petroleum products refining, or brick manufacturing?"

"I can't answer until I have more information, Mr. West. Based on what you have discovered, where do the problems lie and what are the possible returns on investment for each opportunity?"

"A woman after Grandfather's own heart." Charles clapped his hands.

Betsy's interest climbed. Could she become an investor too? After all, she was Daddy Sean's daughter and Corbin's sister. She'd had the same instruction Daddy Sean gave to Corbin, David, and the Bell and Johnson cousins, both male and female. He'd taught them for years in their home, and encouraged them to become as educated as they could. Mother and Josie also expected all the students under Daddy Sean's tutelage to apply their education and become thinkers.

"The ship building industry is changing, Leah. We built fast clipper ships to handle the gold shipments and cargo needs after the California gold rush, but this trade has yielded only normal profits. We also lost maritime trade to New York.

"Iron hulls are popular now, so boilerplate and machine shops are growing. With the news coming out of Europe, especially Germany, the steel industry may gear for war."

"War?" Corbin frowned.

"Yes. The Kaiser seems to have ambitions to control North Africa and Turkey, and to build a navy large enough to challenge Britain."

"What has that got to do with us, Grandfather? We don't involve ourselves with European affairs." Betsy's frown matched Corbin's.

"We will be involved in some way, mark my words, so we need to watch for opportunities."

"Tell me about the other possibilities, Mr. West."

"Since you're going to be family, Leah, call me Grandfather or William. I prefer Grandfather."

Leah sat up straighter. "All right, Grandfather."

Betsy listened to the conversation, her mind spinning with ideas, until Rachel summoned them to lunch.

They rose, but Leah put her hand on William's wrist. "Grandfather? Why are the commercial ice businesses losing money?"

"The breweries, packing houses, and other businesses that used a lot of ice in the past are now using artificial refrigeration."

News of Leah and Corbin's engagement turned lunch into a celebration. The noise reminded Betsy of Christmas Day excitement.

Matthew sat beside her and slid his hand under the table to clasp hers. "Quite a day. Saw you, Leah, Corbin, and Charles talking with your grandfather. What captured your attention for so long?"

Betsy summarized their discussions and the investment opportunities Grandfather presented to Leah.

"You're thinking of investing too?" Matthew released her hand to pass a platter.

"Yes. I'd like to bring something to our marriage besides me."

"You are enough."

Betsy turned to him. "You object?"

Matthew remained silent for several moments. "No, I don't object. I expect to provide for you and our children, though extra money can come in handy. Be careful. Investments can be risky."

"Yes, I know. Don't worry, Matt. Grandfather is wise. Though risk is involved, he knows how to navigate them." She squeezed his elbow. "I'll make certain to talk things over with you. You can help me decide."

The conversation turned to the land Leah wanted to buy.

"Why don't we ride out and take a look at this place?" William turned to Leah. "How long a ride?"

"Two hours. We'd have to leave first thing tomorrow. We don't have enough time today to get there and back before dark."

"I want to go too." Rachel spoke, then slid her gaze to Charles.

He and others echoed her words.

"Best be takin' the wagons for those who don't want to ride." Jim Bell looked at Dwight, Jonathan, and Jesse. They nodded. The women made plans to pack lunches and blankets.

Betsy watched the women and men she'd known all her life with new eyes. These people had traveled the Oregon Trail and survived the Civil War. They'd faced dangers she couldn't imagine. She hoped she was as brave, as she faced her new life as a married woman.

"Where's Deborah? I haven't seen her for awhile." Mary looked around.

Betsy stood. "I saw her go upstairs. I'll get her."

Matt also got to his feet. "The men are going outside for chores. I'll see you later, Betsy." He grabbed his coat and hat.

Betsy opened the door to her bedroom and stopped. Deborah had pulled the small table to the window and spread the journals and letters in front of her. Her index finger marked her place.

She looked up, her eyes wide. "Did you know Lexie Logan knew the future, Betsy?"

Betsy nodded. "Leah and I discovered this last night. We thought she might be an angel or other supernatural being. But she's not."

Deborah frowned. "If not, what is she?"

"A visitor from more than one hundred and fifty years in the future. That's why she knew what was going to happen."

Deborah stared. "A time-traveler? Do you know how incredible this sounds, Bets?"

"Yes, which is why I think our people don't talk about her except among themselves. When you get a chance, look at the necklace your mother gave Leah for Christmas. Lexie gave this to Mary on her sixteenth birthday. Look at the inscription on the back. Lexie received the necklace from her parents for her twenty-second birthday—in 2014."

"What!"

Betsy wheeled around at the special knock. Susana, Rachel, Sarah, and Polly slipped into the room and closed the door.

"Deborah, your mother is looking for you." Susana walked to the table and looked over her cousin's shoulder.

Deborah rose and left, but Susana sat in her place and reached for a journal.

Betsy watched as the other girls took the letters and journals and found comfortable places to read. She waited until she heard the gasps and questions, then shared what she and Leah had discovered.

Polly stared a Rachel and Sarah. "If Leah is right, and Lexie is a descendant, then I'm guessing she is related to you two more than she is to Susana and me."

"Why?" Rachel picked up a journal.

Betsy nodded. "I think she's right. Everyone who knew Lexie said she could be Olivia's identical twin."

"You know," Sarah frowned, "we're not going to be able to tell anyone about Lexie Logan either. They'd think we were crazy. Imagine boasting to beaux, 'I'm related to a time-traveler.'"

Polly laughed. "They'd leave so fast, the door would slam behind them."

"Why would our relationship to Lexie matter, Bets?" Rachel plopped on the bed.

"Because Leah wants to communicate with her in some way."

All the girls stared.

"How?" Polly snickered. "Telegraph? Or Mr. Bell's telephone?"

"We pass the necklace to each generation of daughters and hope this gets to Lexie."

Sarah held up her fingers as if calculating. "Assuming we each get married and have daughters by the age of twenty, and they do the same, the necklace would travel through seven generations."

Betsy rose and tidied the journals and letters. "Leah and I are going to confront Edna, Jonathan, Dwight, and Daddy Sean soon."

Sarah handed over her small stack. "Why? What more can they tell you about her? What more do we need to know?"

Betsy pursed her lips. "You sound like Cor. Did you read anything that told us how Lexie left? Aren't you even the tiniest bit curious about what she told them of the future? Did what she say influence the decisions they made? If so, their choices would indirectly influence us, right?"

"I suppose, but I'd advise you to be cautious about confronting my pa. He doesn't like to be cornered."

Betsy nodded. "I know, Sarah. Jonathan will probably be the most resistant to answering, because he seems to be the one most deeply impacted by Lexie Logan."

I hope our plan doesn't explode in our faces. The thought made Betsy reconsider.

Chapter Ten:

Confrontation

Leah Johnson
Parents: Jesse Johnson and Mary Bell Johnson
Siblings: William, Zach, Deborah
Uncle, Aunt, Cousins: Jonathan, Olivia, Rachel, Sarah
Uncle, Aunt, Cousins: Dwight, Josie, Susana, Polly
Uncle, Grandparents: Matthew, Edna, Jim Bell, Nate Johnson

We left when the sun topped the horizon. The rays touched the crystal snow diamonds and made them sparkle.

All of the Johnson, Bell, and West family members decided to come, so the outing took on the sound and feel of a winter picnic. The snow was not deep enough to cause problems for the wagons or the riders, so we picked up the pace when we could.

Laughter and song seemed to shorten our two hour journey.

"Do you remember when we rode back from the Clarks' after the tornado, Jon?" Sean lowered his voice, and I turned my head to hear from my position in front of them. I pretended to study the sky and trees as I rode next to Corbin.

Uncle Jon chuckled. "Yes. She sang so many songs we couldn't get a word in edge-wise. I think she did this on purpose."

I could hear the warmth in Sean's voice. "I know she did. If she sang, we couldn't talk—or fight."

She. Lexie Logan. I sure wanted to communicate with her.

The property came into view, so I stopped and pointed.

Several of my cousins hopped out of the wagons and each mounted behind one of the riders so they could continue where the wagons couldn't.

Charles offered a stirrup for Rachel, who mounted behind him with ease and grace. He was a better rider than I expected for a man from the city. Will helped Sarah mount behind him. Sarah winked at me and put her arms around my brother's waist. Will pulled her closer and patted her gloved hand.

Grandma Edna, Olivia, Josie, Laura, and Annie said they'd stay and get the picnic lunch ready, so we turned off the trail and spent the next two hours examining the properties.

"When and how did you find this place, Leah?" Corbin glanced around. "I'm surprised others haven't found and filed on the land."

"You have to admit, this is off the beaten path and more isolated than some like. I saw this land many years ago when Grandpa Jim and Uncle Dwight took me with them to help a settler on the other side of the mountain. They thought this might be a short cut." I chuckled. "The trip was actually longer, but I remember how sunny and grassy this place was in the late spring."

"Describe what you envision." He looked around.

I pointed to the left. "I'd graze cattle in the valleys and on the far side of the creek, and I'd fence off pastures for the horses closer to the barn. Do you see how the elevation changes along the creek? I'd like to build spreader dams to use for irrigation. See that knoll in the middle of the property? Near that stand of cottonwoods? I'd put the house there so I'd have a view out any window. I think I'll be able to find water for a well."

Grandpa Nate and William rode up and joined my cousins as I explained. They listened and looked without comment until I finished.

"Not goin' to have any problem findin' lumber for building. I can get my portable saw mill in and set up over there." Grandpa Nate pointed.

My dream took on shape and smelled of pine shavings.

William studied the layout of the land. "I'm impressed, Leah. You've put a lot of thought into planning. The amount of work you'll have to do on this place doesn't scare you?"

"No. I'm used to hard work. I've helped in the smithy, built fence with the men, herded cattle, and trained horses. I know what I'm up against. Besides, the men in my family on both sides are strong and able. They'll help me."

"Yep. Hard to find anybody around stronger than Jim, Dwight, and Matt," Grandpa Nate agreed and patted my arm.

Grandpa Jim, Uncle Dwight, Ma, and Uncle Matt rode up with the Johnson men. Betsy rode behind Uncle Matt, her arms encircling his waist.

I shared my ideas, and they and Grandpa Nate began planning to make my dream a reality. Warmth spread from my center to every part of my body. "If only I could make the years speed up until I turn twenty-one."

Cor nodded and glanced around. "I know. I hope no one finds this place and files before we can."

William remained silent for several moments. "I have a proposition. I'd like you to listen to me until I'm finished before you comment. Agreed?"

We nodded.

"Since Leah, Corbin, and I are going into business together, I'd like to make their dreams a reality sooner than they expect. My suggestion is that I file on the property Leah wants, and Benjamin files on the adjoining property. Once we have the land patents, you all could start building immediately. Then, when Leah and Corbin turn twenty-one, we'll sell the places to them for what we bought the land for."

Benjamin looked out across the property. "I'd be willing to help them out."

"Why would you do this, William?" Suspicion laced Grandpa Nate's words.

"Let's say this is an investment opportunity. I will invest in the lives of my partners."

"What do you expect in return?" Pa frowned.

"Great grandchildren, Jesse. A comfortable place to stay when I visit. The company of family. Business partners who are smart even though they're young."

Pa glanced at Ma, and she nodded.

William crossed his arms. "I'm assuming Leah and Corbin will live on her land when they're married, but Corbin still has to build on his to prove up. Whichever house is not lived in could be a place for visitors to stay. What do you think?"

My thoughts spun like a desert dust devil.

The men waited for me to answer.

"Let me pray about this and talk to Cor, Grandfather."

He raised his eyebrows and took a deep breath. Everyone discussed ideas over the picnic lunch and on the way back to the Aubry ranch. Each had a suggestion or comment and often started their sentence with, "If this were my place, I'd ..."

I gave thanks I had so many people who loved me.

Back at the ranch, the men did outside chores, and the women went in to help with dinner. I stood next to Betsy as we chopped vegetables and whispered, "After dinner?"

She nodded. "You get them in the sitting room, and I'll bring down the letters and journals. Cor said he'd keep as many of the others occupied as he can. He's got the chess board set up for Nate and Grandfather, and he's asked Sarah and Rachel and Susana and Polly to entertain Mother, Aunt Josie, and Cousin Olivia. The boy cousins and brothers are on their own."

"My stomach feels like I've swallowed fighting snakes, Betsy. What if we confront them, and they still won't talk about Lexie? What will we do then?"

"I don't know, but I think we should be humble and honest instead of demanding."

"Yes, especially where Uncle Jon is concerned."

The more I thought about how the upcoming confrontation—no, conversation—could go, the more my fingers trembled.

Corbin reached for my hand under the table and intertwined his fingers with mine. He whispered, "They won't eat you, Leah."

After dinner, I approached Grandma Edna, Ma, Uncle Jon, Uncle Dwight, and Sean and asked them if we could talk. They nodded and followed me to the sitting room.

Betsy entered with the letters and journals and Uncle Matthew on her heels. She sat down next to me. "One of his letters to Mary fell out of the journal. He recognized some of the letters and got suspicious, Leah. I'm sorry."

"What's this about?" Grandma Edna looked from me to Betsy to Ma.

I swallowed the lump in my throat and glanced at each of them. "Do you trust me? Do you trust Betsy?"

Sean frowned. "Of course. Why?"

I looked at Uncle Jon. "Do you think either one of us would cause you deliberate pain?"

His jaw hardened. "I don't like where I think you're headed, Leah."

Uncle Matt sucked in a breath. "Lexie."

"Yes, Lexie. Please don't shut us out. We know you've made promises not to talk about her with others, but we want to show you something." I handed a letter to Ma. "Do you recognize your letter?"

She looked at the date and signature and nodded.

"Sean, is this your letter to Ma?"

He read a few sentences and nodded. "Where did you get these?"

"In a trunk in the attic."

"Get to the point, Leah." Uncle Jonathan waited, his body tense.

"The point is when you all stopped talking about Lexie Logan every time we came around, Betsy, my cousins, and I felt you didn't trust us. We wondered what you were hiding. At one point in our investigation, we thought at least one of you was indirectly responsible for her death."

Their eyes widened and they stared at me as if I had suddenly grown extra limbs.

"Her death?" Uncle Dwight laughed without humor.

"An investigation?" Sean leaned forward and put his forearms on his thighs. "Explain."

I did, but stopped before I shared our belief Lexie was from the future. "We no longer think any of you were involved in foul play."

"That relieves our minds, I'm sure. What do you believe?" A trace of sarcasm tinged Sean's words.

I picked up the letters and journals and read from their own writing. "We now believe Lexie Logan was a time-traveler from the twenty-first century. We also believe she is a descendant of yours and Olivia's, Uncle Jonathan."

"What?" They all spoke as one. Uncle Jon paled.

"Do you admit Lexie is a time-traveler? Don't worry, we won't tell anyone. They'd think we were crazy. We've agreed not to talk about her to others also."

Uncle Matt looked from Betsy and me to the others. "Might as well tell them so we can get some peace from their questions and suspicions."

"What do you want to know?" Uncle Jon's words were clipped.

I looked at Betsy. Her smile encouraged me, so I continued, "How did Lexie get to 1857?"

Grandma Edna answered, "God sent her. Wanted her to learn some lessons. Jim and me found her sleepin' like a baby on the prairie. She didn't know nothin' about nothin' when she woke up. Prayed every day God would be sendin' her back home."

"She brought things with her from the future." Ma fidgeted. "A thing she called a phone that took movin' pictures and recorded our voices."

"Don't forget that iPod, Mary." Uncle Matt describe the small object that allowed them all, especially great grandpa Fergus to enjoy listening to a full symphony.

Sean looked at me. "She knew about the war. Lexie described the devastation and the outcome, and what she told us influenced our move to Oregon."

Grandma Edna, Ma, Uncle Dwight, and Uncle Mattie nodded.

Ma brushed at a tear. "As you read in my letter to your pa, Lexie knew the date and place Lee surrendered."

Uncle Jon spoke in a low voice, "She knew the date and place President Lincoln would be assassinated and named his assassin."

"She quoted the first part of Lincoln's Gettysburg address years before the Battle of Gettysburg." Uncle Dwight grimaced.

My eyes widened. "What happened to Lexie Logan, Ma?"

Uncle Jonathan straightened and turned to look at Ma.

Ma seemed to understand his sudden interest, because she said, "We told y'all the truth. Lexie poured out her heart to God as she played the piano. Seems she finally understood why the good Lord sent her to us. She cried and asked for forgiveness and a second chance, and a moment later, all we saw were the clothes she wore. Good thing she wore her twenty-first century clothes underneath."

Grandma Edna nodded. "That be the truth Jonathan."

"I was there too, remember?" Uncle Matthew's eyes met those of Uncle Jonathan's. "I know what I saw, Jon. First, Lexie was there, then she wasn't. You, Jesse, and Nate came in right after and searched within minutes of her snatching."

Uncle Dwight frowned. "Are you satisfied, Leah?"

I glanced at Betsy. She looked at the papers in her lap before she nodded.

"For the most part. We're still interested in her as a person and the details of her time with you all. If we promise not to talk about Lexie Logan to anyone who doesn't know she's a time-traveler, will you promise to tell us more about her if we ask?"

They looked at each other. Uncle Jonathan stood. "Yes."

The rest of them echoed his word or nodded.

We stood also and turned to follow Jon out of the room.

Uncle Matt put his arm around Betsy's waist and cinched her to his side. "I'm glad I don't have to be so careful with my words now, Bets."

"Me too. One of these days, I want to hear all the details."

He groaned. "That will take hours."

Betsy cocked her head and looked in his eyes. "What better way to spend winter nights after we're married?"

"I had something different in mind, but I promise to tell you everything I remember about Lexie Logan. Deal?"

"Deal."

Corbin stood outside the door. He whispered near my ear. "Grab your coat and a blanket. The porch swing awaits."

We wrapped ourselves in the heavy blanket, and I snuggled next to him. "Today has been the best day of my life."

"Yes, mine too." He rested his cheek on the top of my head. "What do you think of Grandfather's proposal?"

I sat up and looked in his eyes. "The more I think of his plan, the more excited I get. We can start felling logs for the houses and barns and let them season as soon as William and Ben have the titles in hand. We can't dig the wells or build fence until the spring thaw, but we can cut the posts and rails and have them ready to go.

"My cousins, aunts, and Grandma Edna all like to sew. If I provide them with material, they could start curtains and bedding once we know how many bedrooms and windows." I pushed the swing faster in my enthusiasm. "I'll purchase the material in Boston if I can find what I want."

Corbin slowed the swing and drew the blanket tighter around us. "I'm sure Grandfather knows an architect or two we can consult about the plans." His breath turned frosty in the cold night air.

"You and I need to talk about what we want for the properties before we talk to the architects."

"Good idea." He looked at the stars and then at me. "Are you now satisfied our family members aren't murderers?"

"Yes, but I'm determined to make contact with Lexie some how. The more I find out about her, the more I like her. Though time separates us, I think she's my kind of person."

Cor turned and stared at me. "How do you propose to reach her, since she won't be born for another century and a half?"

"I'm going to ask the cousins to help me, especially Rachel and Sarah. I think each of us should be photographed wearing the necklace. We'll put our names, date, and a short note on the back of each picture.

"We'll pass the tradition on to our daughters and granddaughters, who will continue with their daughters and granddaughters—I hope. I think we should also stress they should keep the photos with Olivia's journals and the letters. When either Rachel or Sarah has a daughter, I'll gift the necklace to the eldest daughter."

"You intend to tell these future women who Lexie is?"

"No. Hopefully, they'll pass on the traditions without asking questions."

"Like you, Betsy, and the cousins?"

"Point taken." I rested my head on his shoulder. "Knowing the Johnson legacy continues into the future makes me wonder what we'll pass down, Cor."

He pushed the swing and reached for my hand. "How about faith, love, integrity, and loyalty?"

"A worthy legacy. Now kiss me before we go inside."

He obliged.

About the Author

DERINDA BABCOCK is an author and graphic designer. She lives in southwestern Colorado near the base of the western slope of the Rocky Mountains.

In her previous career as an English as a Second Language teacher, she worked with students of all ages and many different linguistic and cultural backgrounds. The richness of this experience lends flavor and voice to the stories she writes.

When Derinda is not writing or designing, she continues her education. You can contact her at www.derindababcock.com/contact

Derinda's Other Books

Elk Lake Publishing, Inc.
The Destiny Trilogy
Dodging Destiny
In Search of Destiny
Hunting for Destiny (novella)
Following Destiny
Voices from the Past (short novella)

BOOK 1   BOOK 2   NOVELLA   BOOK 3   SHORT STORY

Treasures of the Heart trilogy:
Colorado Treasure
Trouble in Texas (2021)
The Prodigal Returns (2022)

A Tale of Three Kingdoms trilogy:

The Jindentors
The Vindorans (2021)
The Binromese (2022)

Made in the USA
Columbia, SC
14 December 2022

73987100R00072